ADVENTURES iN MAKERSPACE

A LOW-TECH MISSiON

WRITTEN BY
SHANNON MCCLINTOCK MILLER
AND
BLAKE HOENA

ILLUSTRATED BY
ALAN BROWN

STONE ARCH BOOKS
a capstone imprint

MEET THE SPECIALIST

ABILITIES:
speed reader, tech titan,
foreign language master,
traveler through literature
and history

MS. GILLIAN
TEACHER-LIBRARIAN

MEET THE STUDENTS

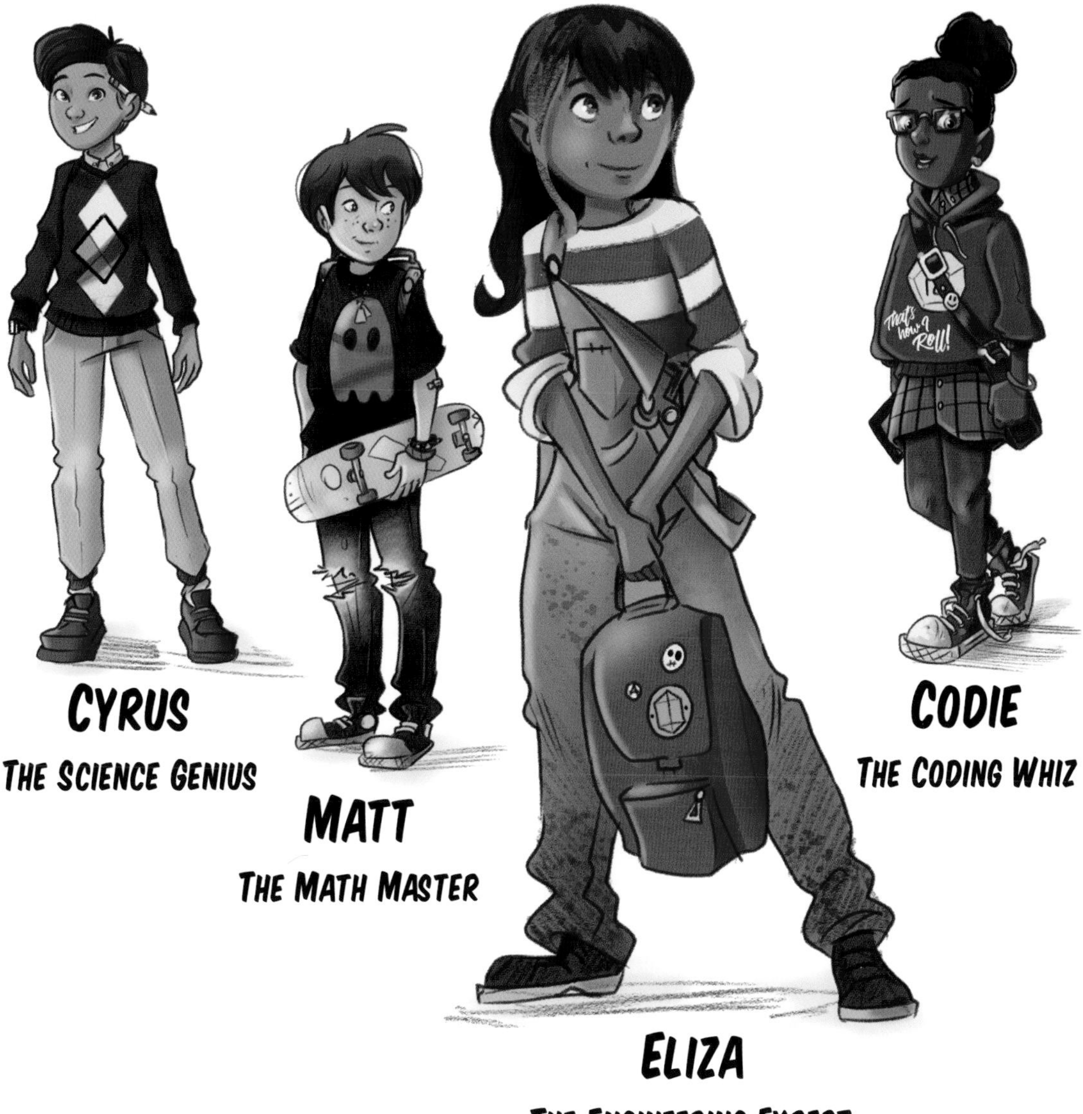
That's how I Roll!

CYRUS

THE SCIENCE GENIUS

MATT

THE MATH MASTER

ELIZA

THE ENGINEERING EXPERT

CODIE

THE CODING WHIZ

THE CHALLENGE

ELIZA AND HER FRIENDS ARE ALWAYS EXCITED TO VISIT THE LIBRARY. IT IS THEIR FAVORITE PLACE IN ALL OF EMERSON ELEMENTARY. AT THE BACK OF THE LIBRARY IS AN AREA THAT MS. GILLIAN CALLS THE MAKERSPACE.

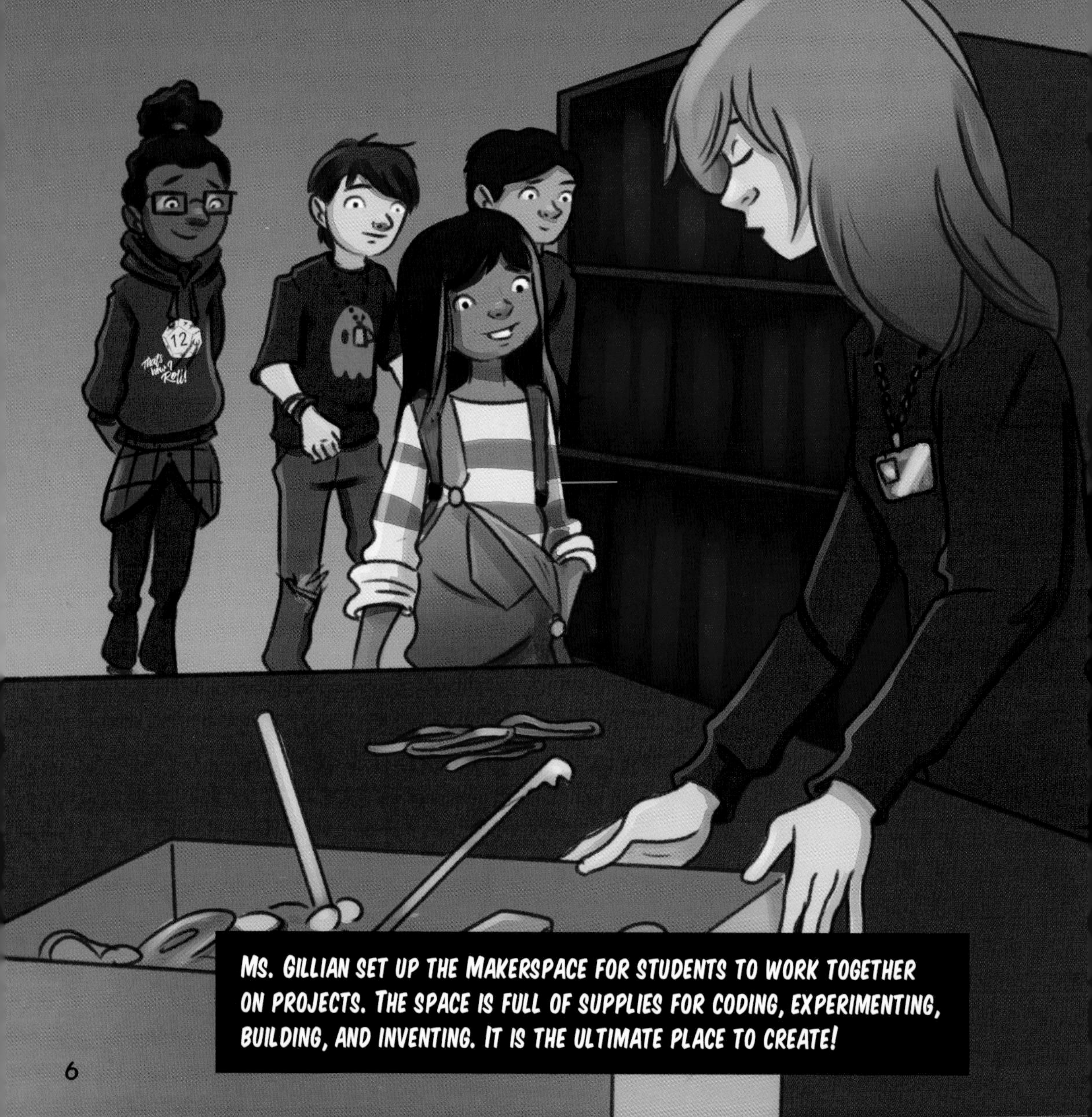
MS. GILLIAN SET UP THE MAKERSPACE FOR STUDENTS TO WORK TOGETHER ON PROJECTS. THE SPACE IS FULL OF SUPPLIES FOR CODING, EXPERIMENTING, BUILDING, AND INVENTING. IT IS THE ULTIMATE PLACE TO CREATE!

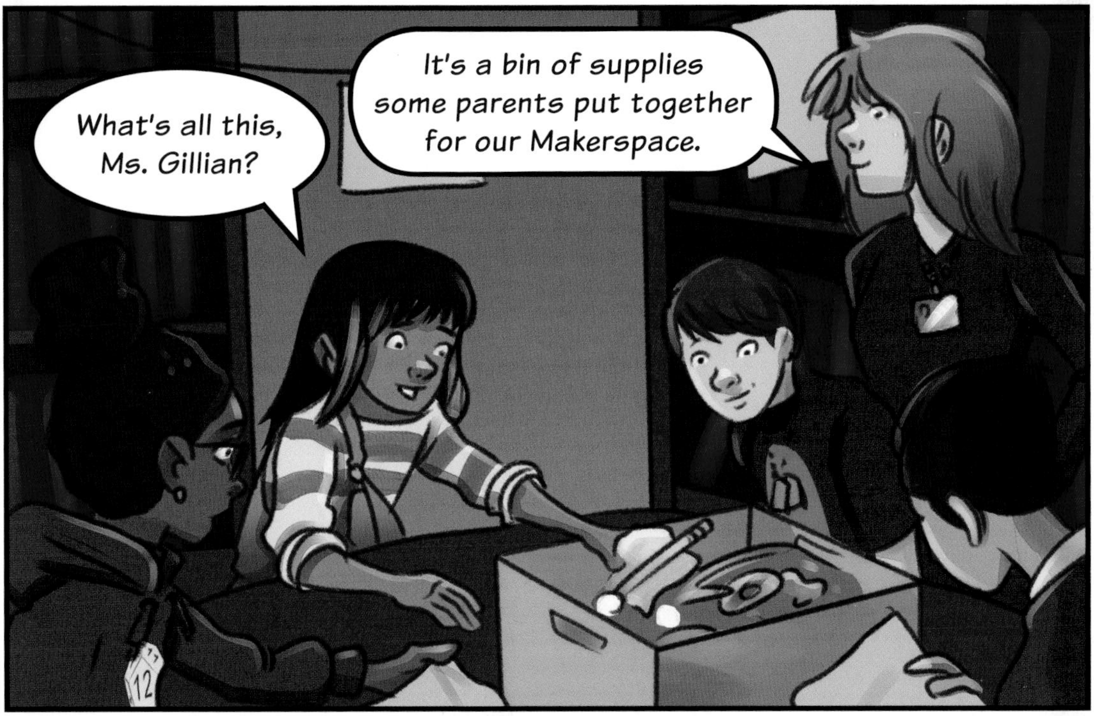
What's all this, Ms. Gillian?
It's a bin of supplies some parents put together for our Makerspace.
12

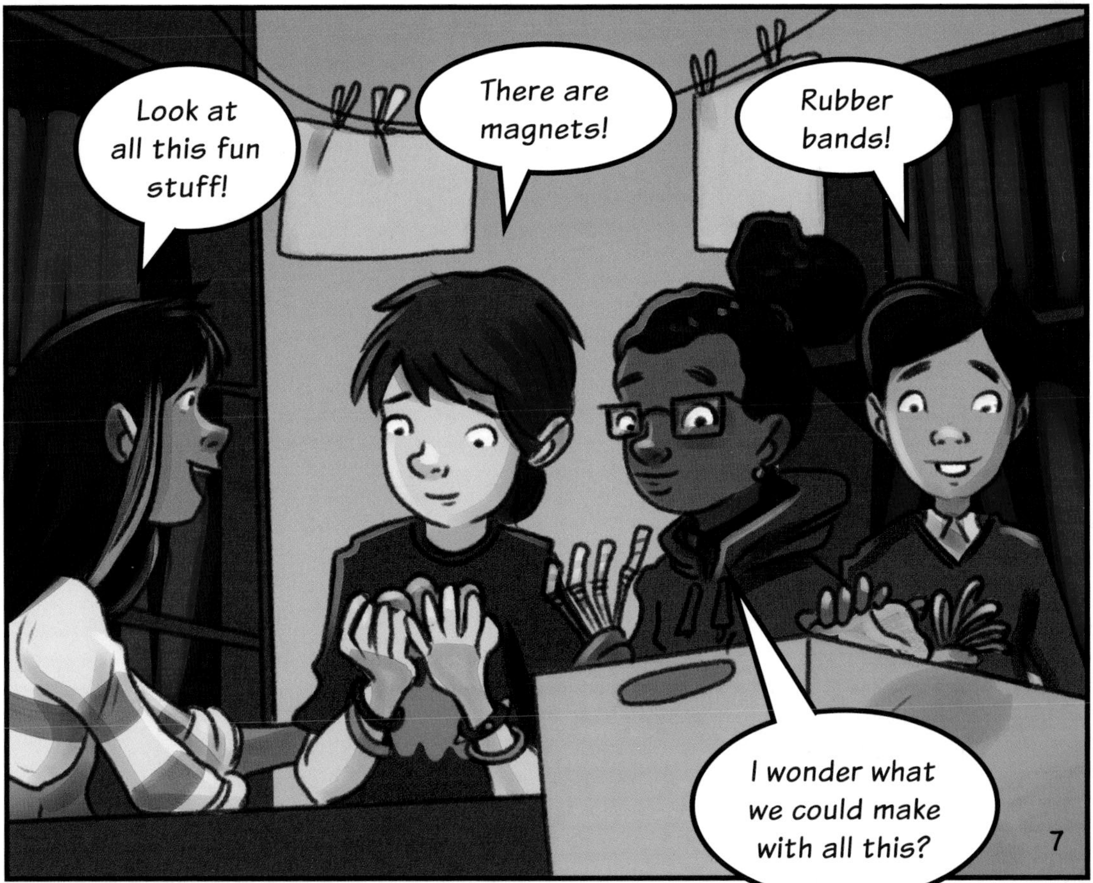
Look at all this fun stuff!
There are magnets!
Rubber bands!
I wonder what we could make with all this?

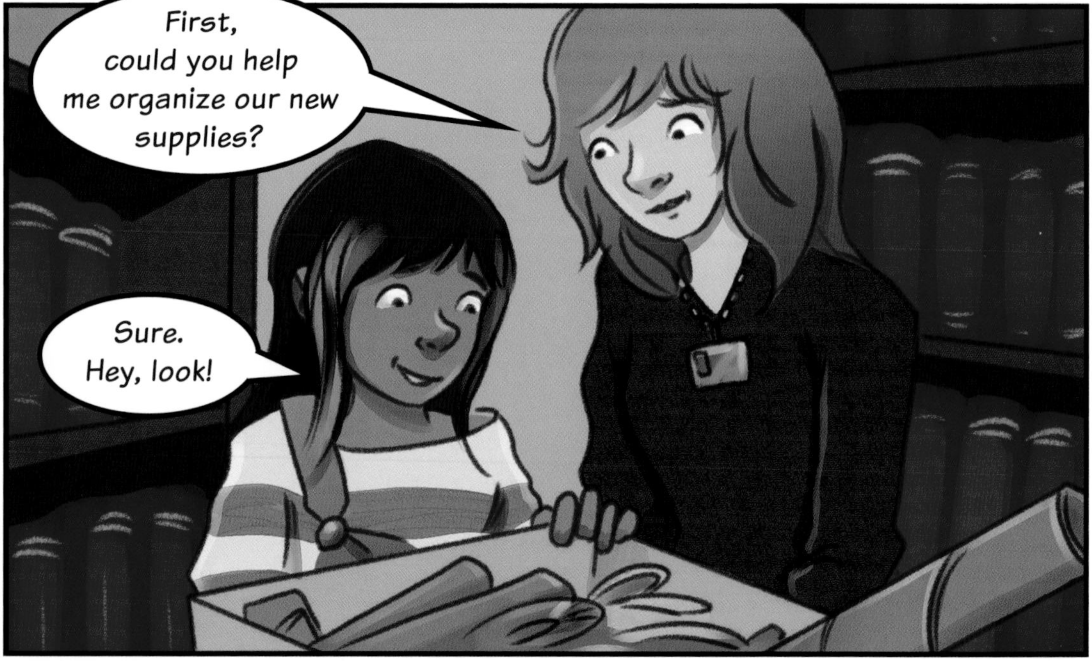
First, could you help me organize our new supplies?
Sure. Hey, look!

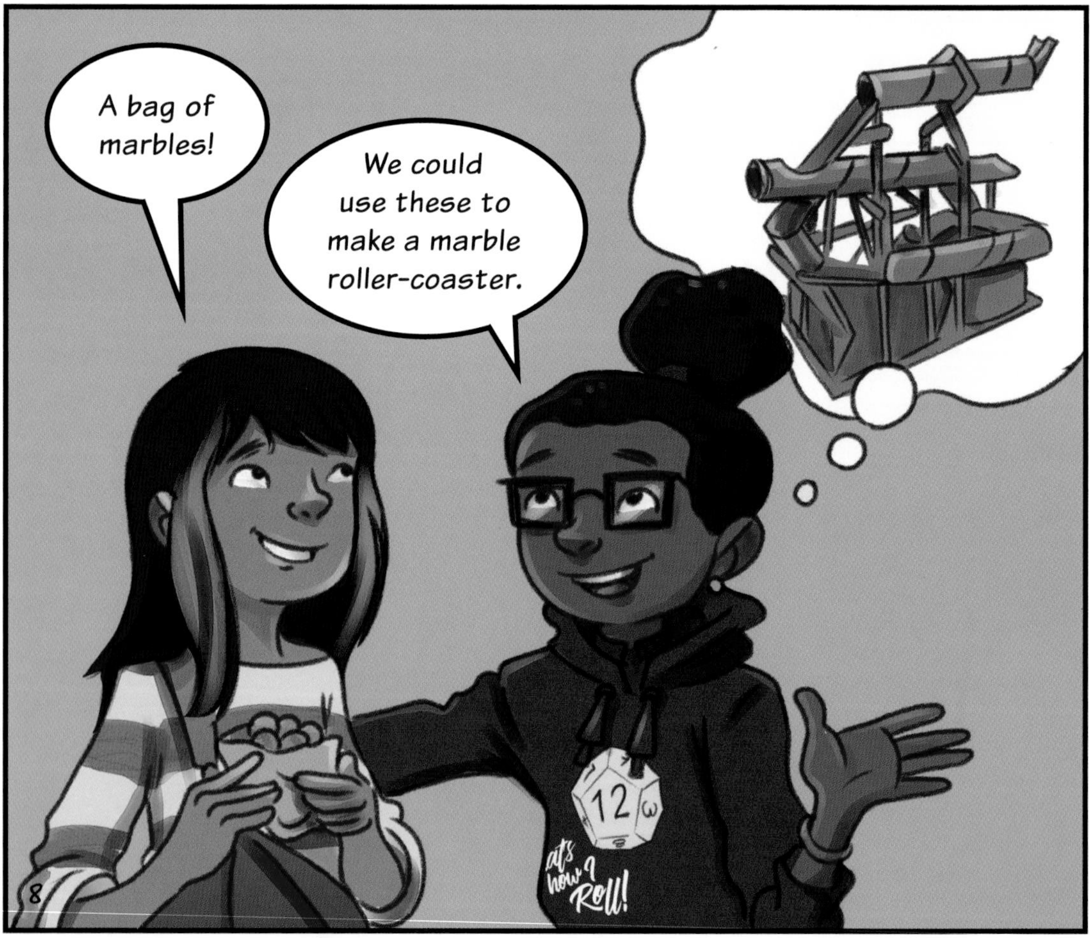
A bag of marbles!
We could use these to make a marble roller-coaster.
12

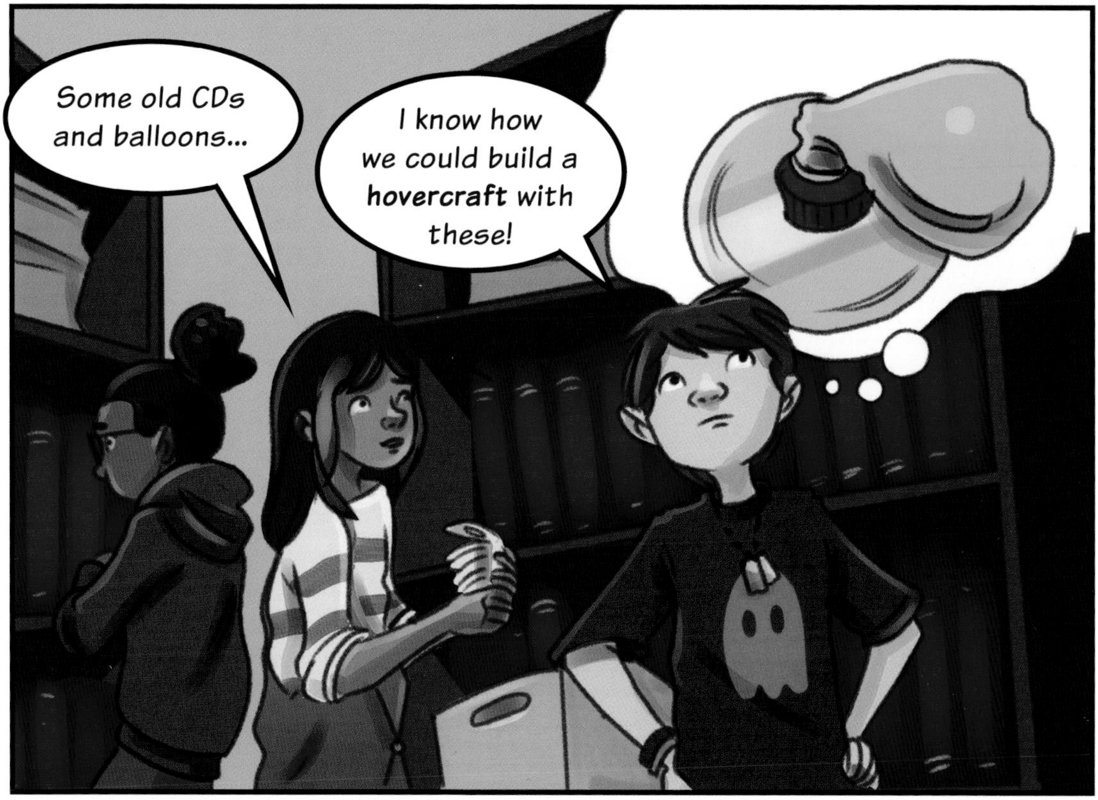
Some old CDs and balloons...
I know how we could build a **hovercraft** with these!

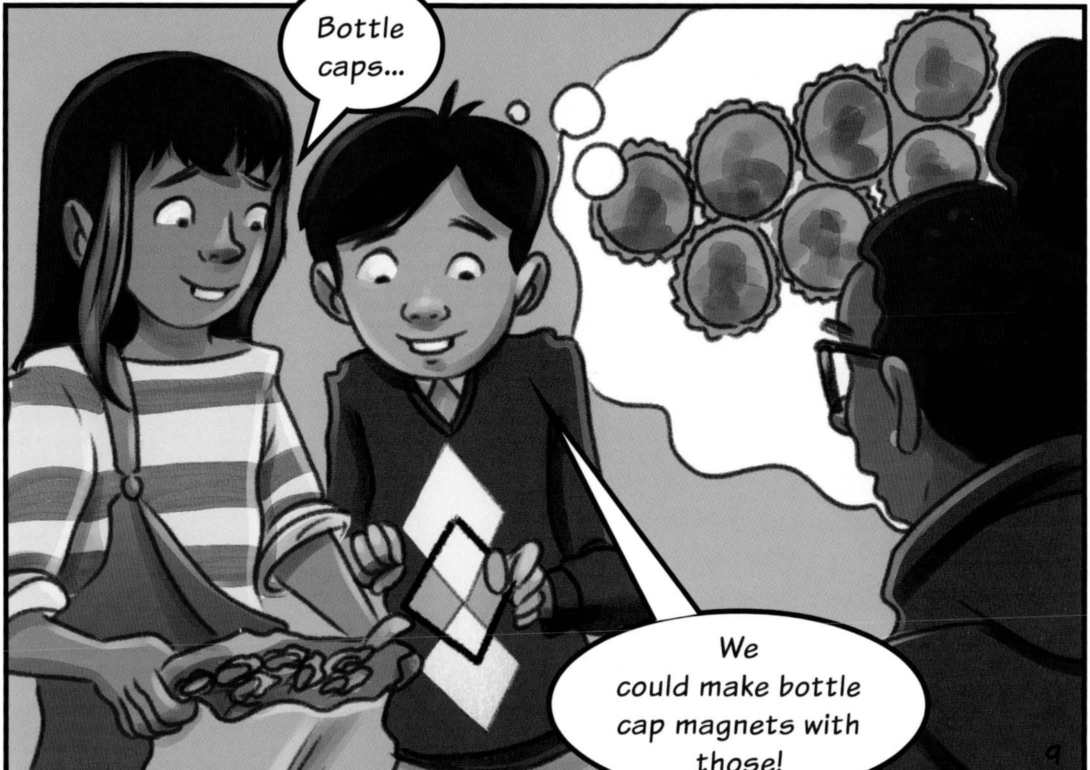
Bottle caps...
We could make bottle cap magnets with those!

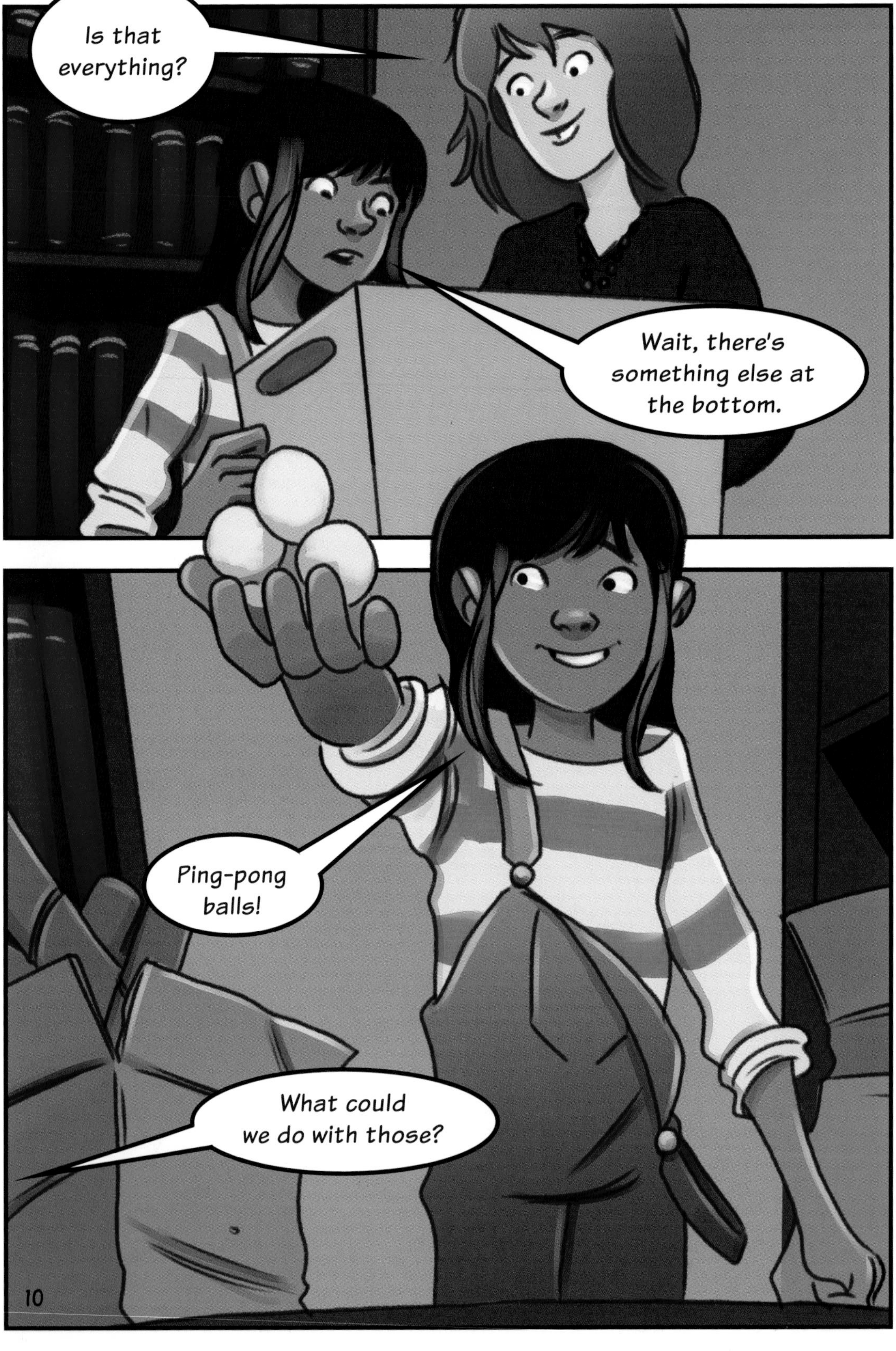
Is that everything?
Wait, there's something else at the bottom.
Ping-pong balls!
What could we do with those?

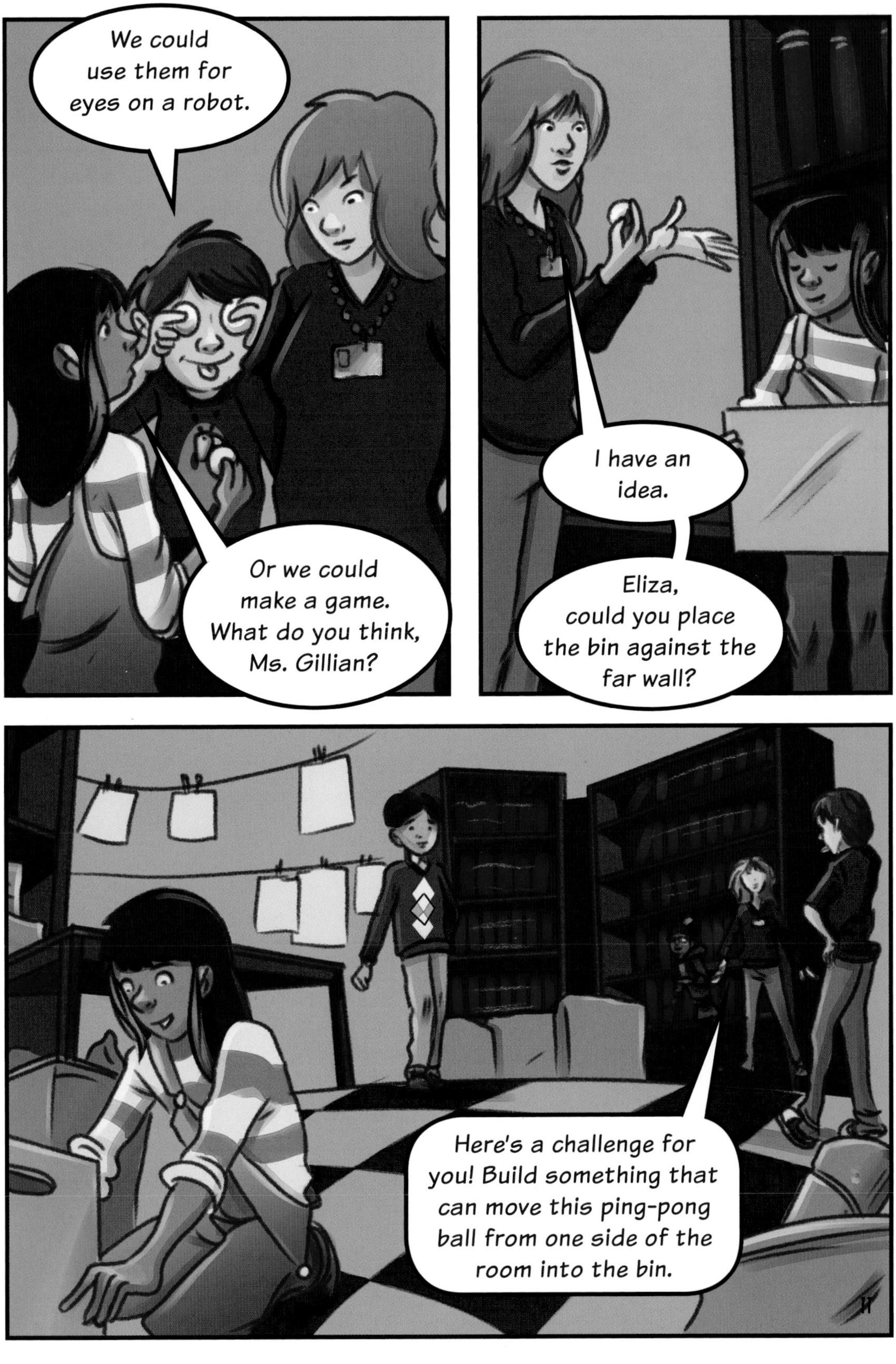
We could use them for eyes on a robot.
Or we could make a game. What do you think, Ms. Gillian?
I have an idea.
Eliza, could you place the bin against the far wall?
Here's a challenge for you! Build something that can move this ping-pong ball from one side of the room into the bin.

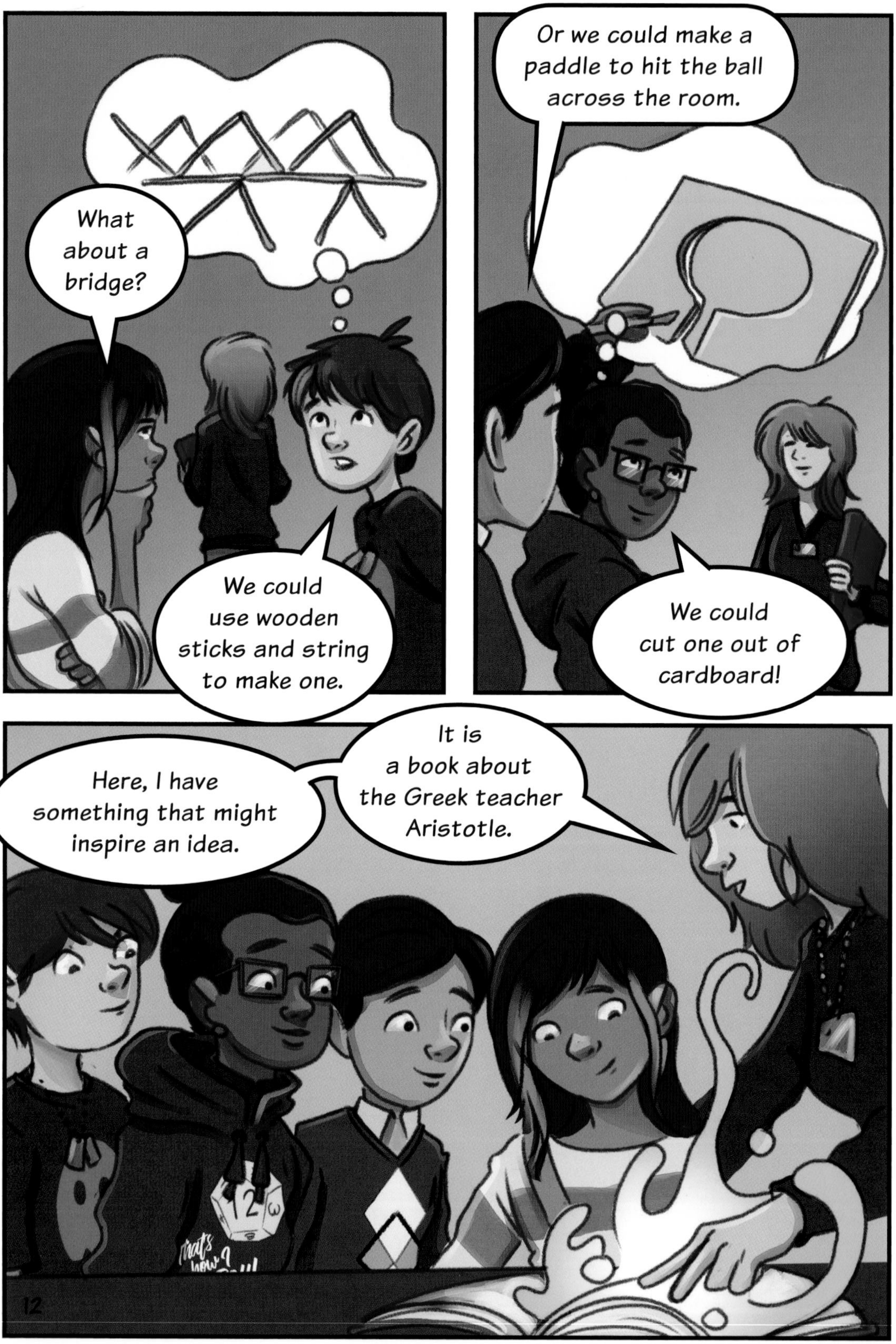
What about a bridge?
We could use wooden sticks and string to make one.
Or we could make a paddle to hit the ball across the room.
We could cut one out of cardboard!
Here, I have something that might inspire an idea.
It is a book about the Greek teacher Aristotle.

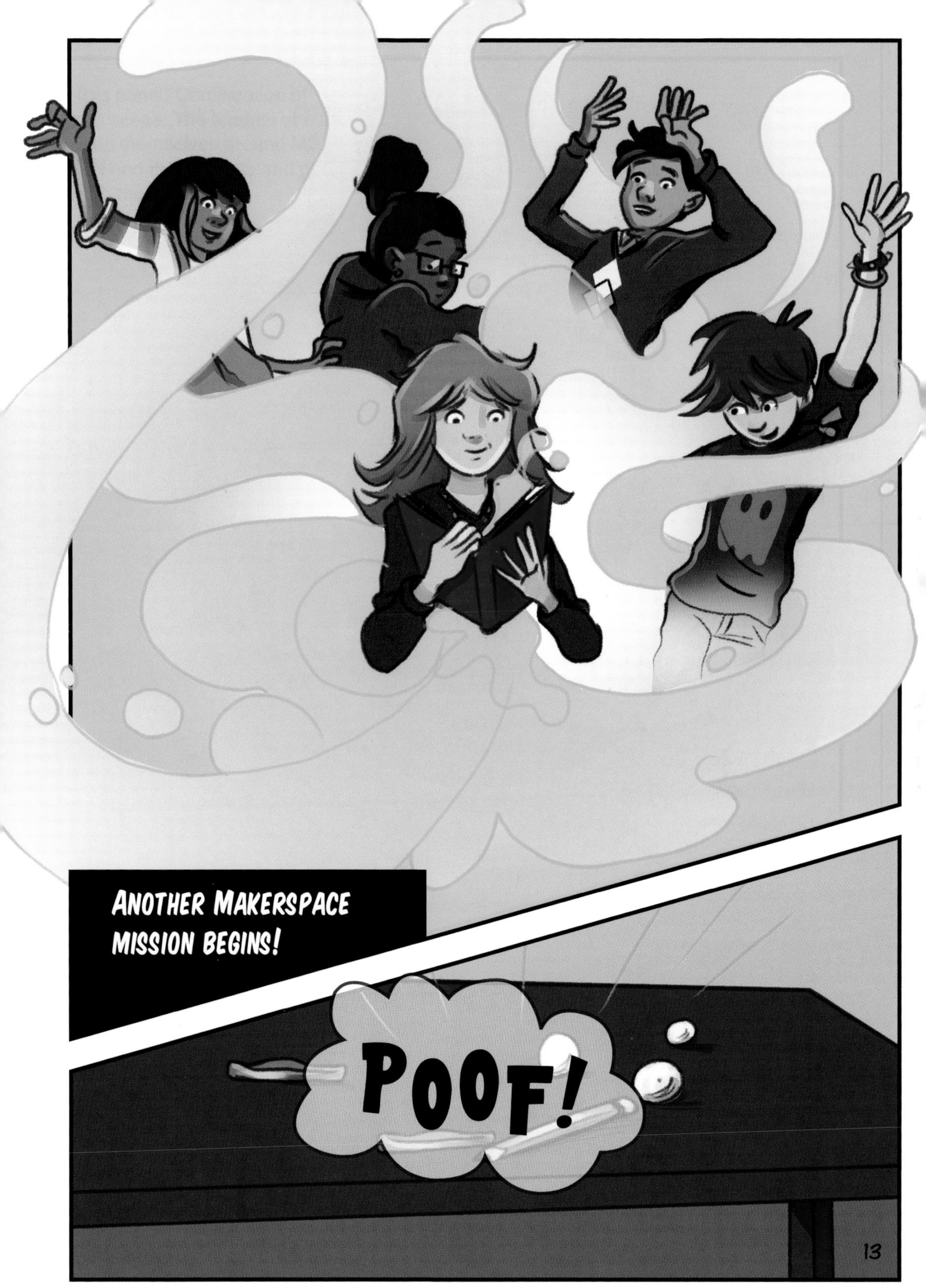
ANOTHER MAKERSPACE MISSION BEGINS!
POOF!

THE BATTLE OF JAXARTES

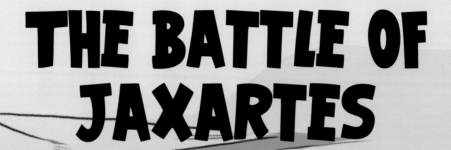

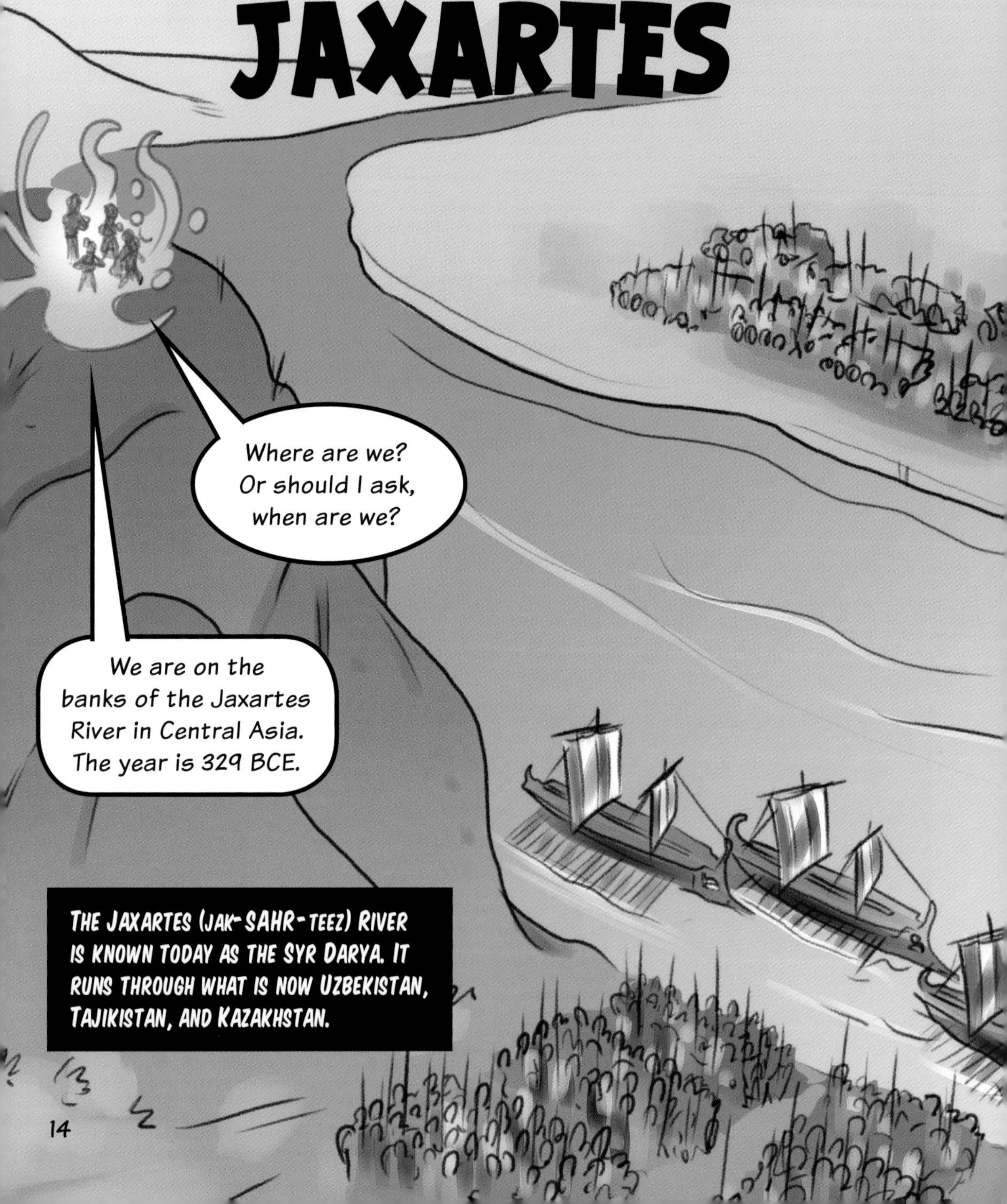
Where are we? Or should I ask, when are we?
We are on the banks of the Jaxartes River in Central Asia. The year is 329 BCE.
THE JAXARTES (JAK-SAHR-TEEZ) RIVER IS KNOWN TODAY AS THE SYR DARYA. IT RUNS THROUGH WHAT IS NOW UZBEKISTAN, TAJIKISTAN, AND KAZAKHSTAN.

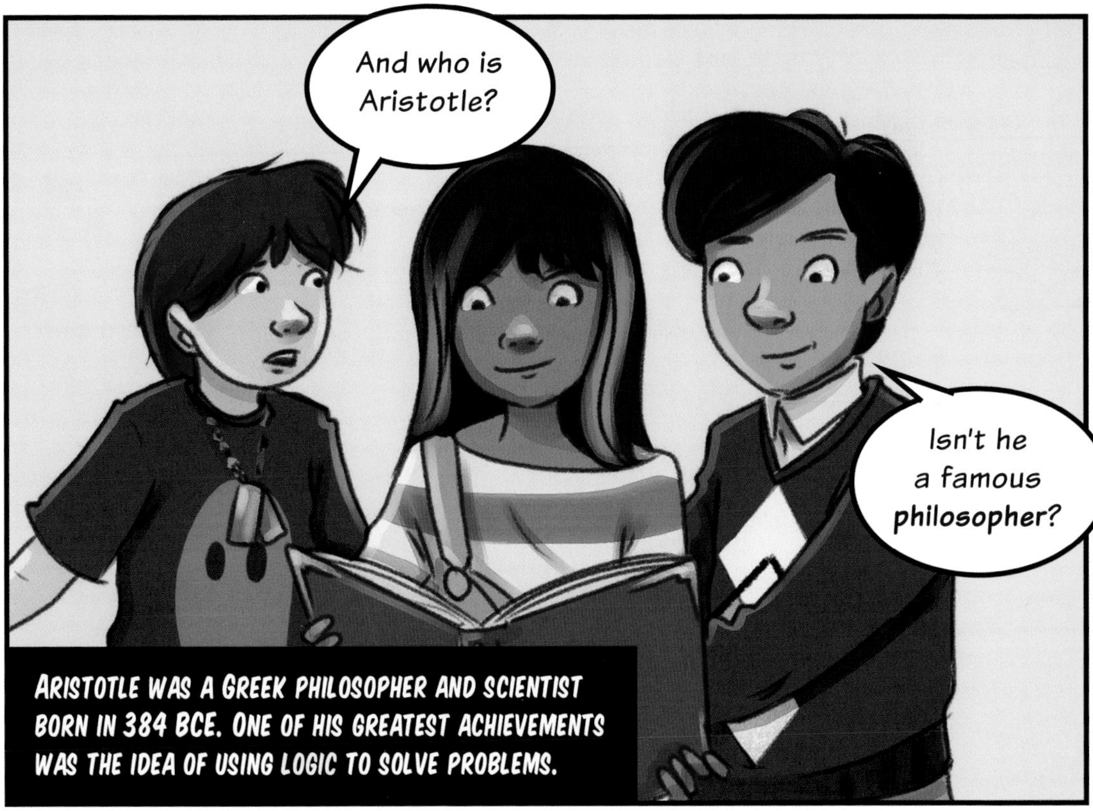
And who is Aristotle?
Isn't he a famous **philosopher**?
ARISTOTLE WAS A GREEK PHILOSOPHER AND SCIENTIST BORN IN 384 BCE. ONE OF HIS GREATEST ACHIEVEMENTS WAS THE IDEA OF USING LOGIC TO SOLVE PROBLEMS.

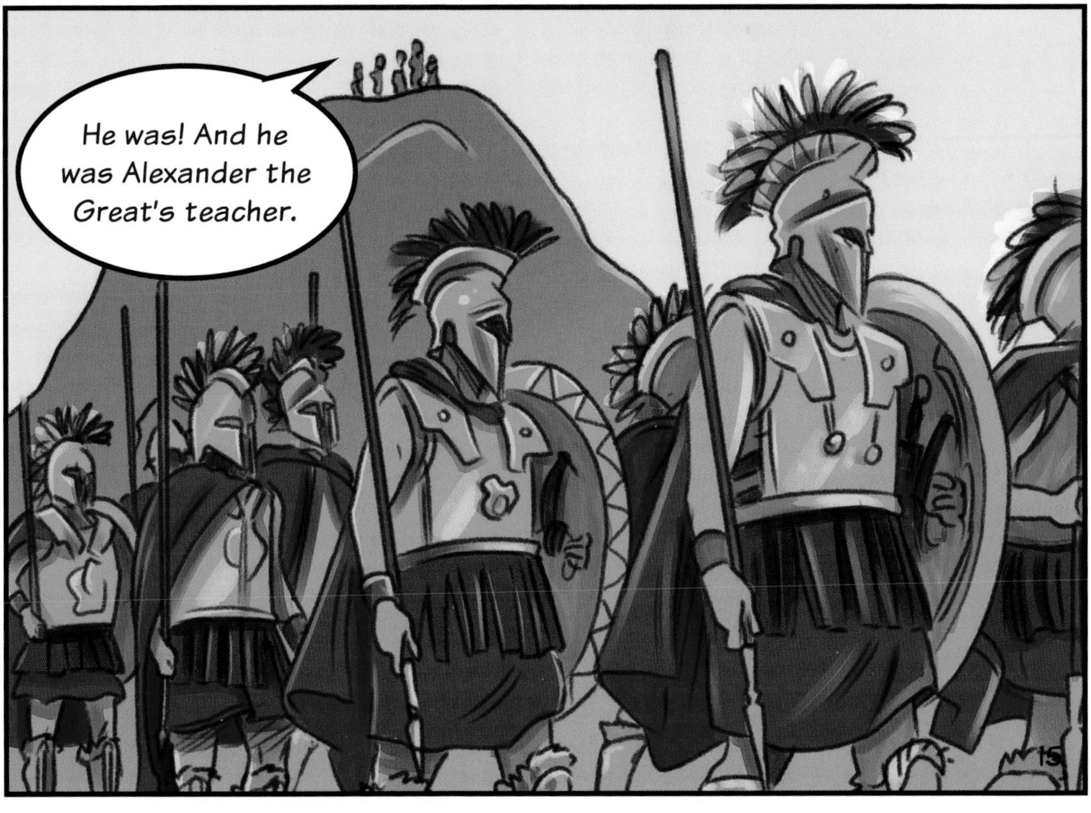
He was! And he was Alexander the Great's teacher.

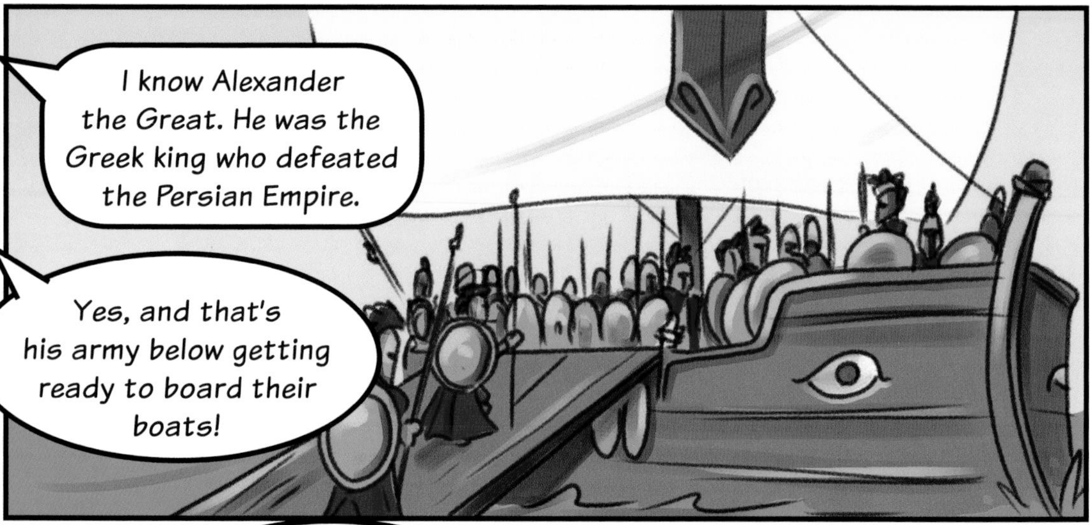
I know Alexander the Great. He was the Greek king who defeated the Persian Empire.
Yes, and that's his army below getting ready to board their boats!

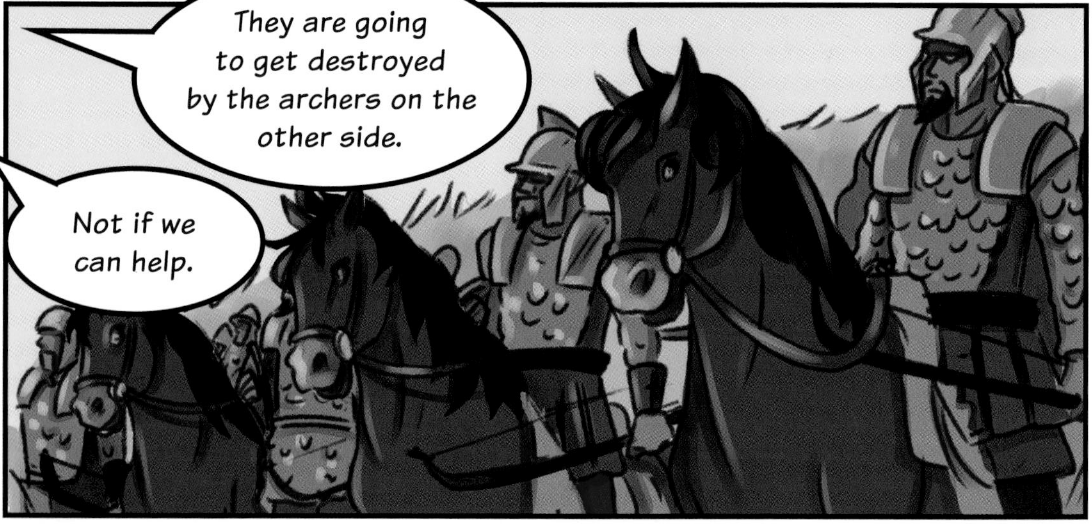
They are going to get destroyed by the archers on the other side.
Not if we can help.

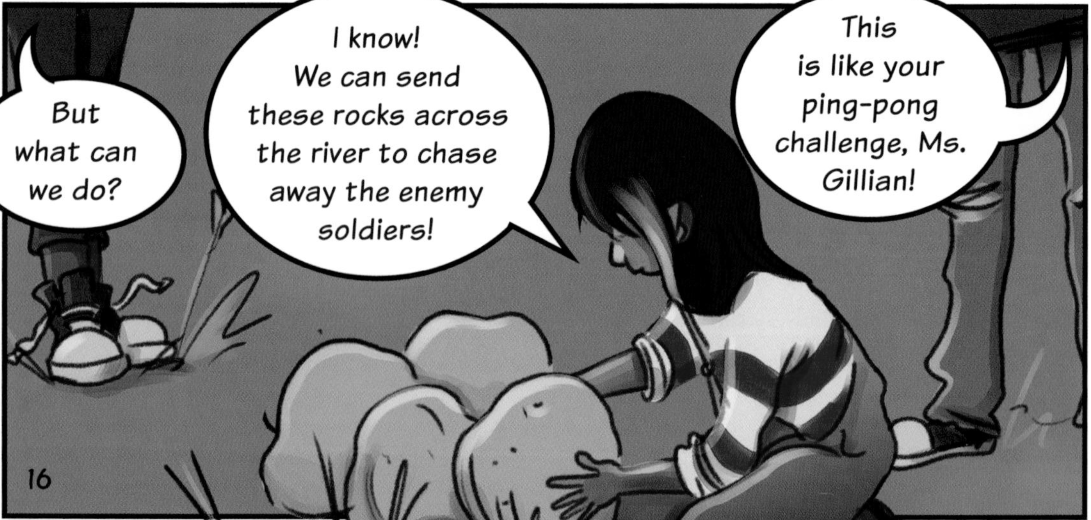
But what can we do?
I know! We can send these rocks across the river to chase away the enemy soldiers!
This is like your ping-pong challenge, Ms. Gillian!

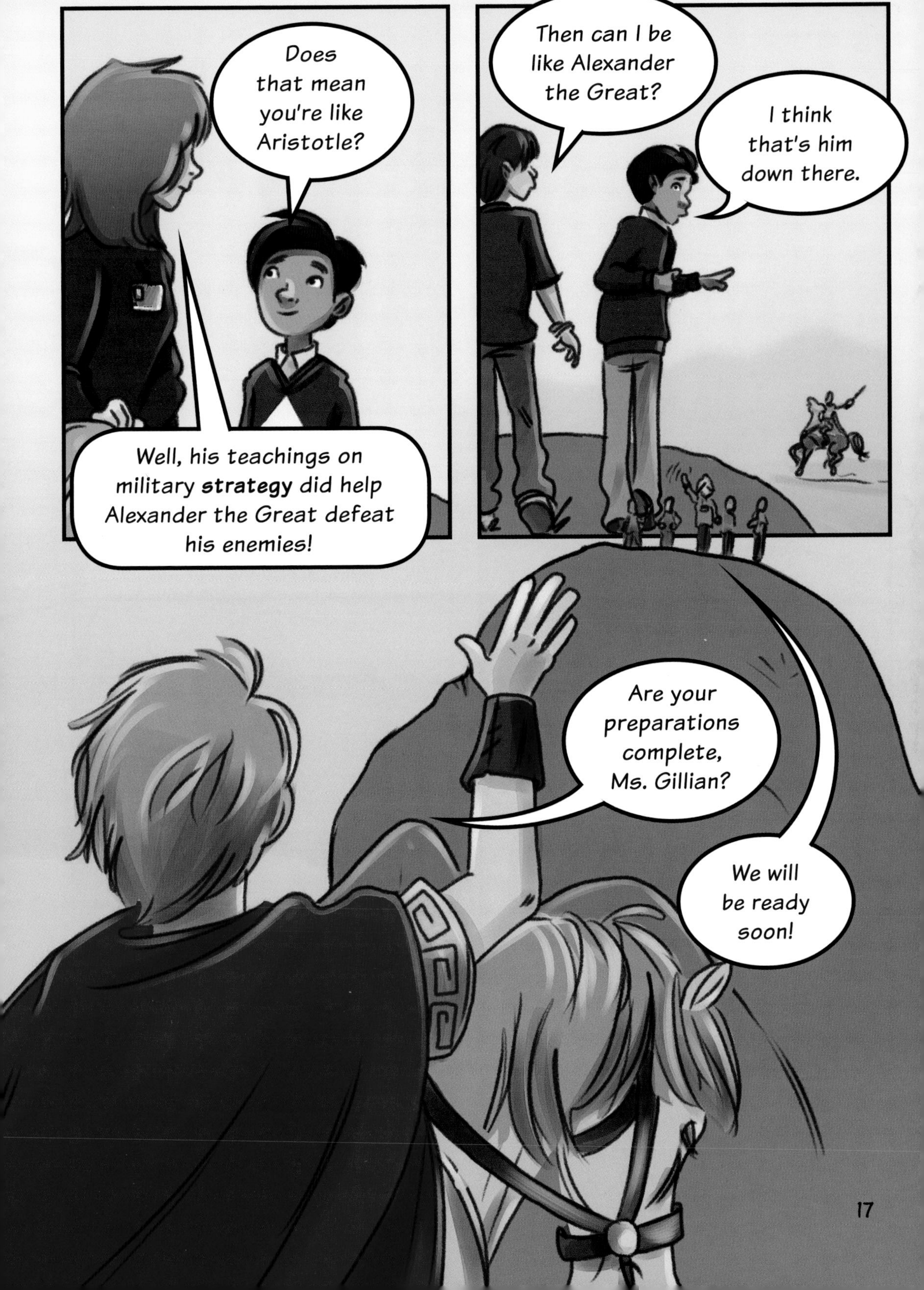
Does that mean you're like Aristotle?
Well, his teachings on military **strategy** did help Alexander the Great defeat his enemies!
Then can I be like Alexander the Great?
I think that's him down there.
Are your preparations complete, Ms. Gillian?
We will be ready soon!

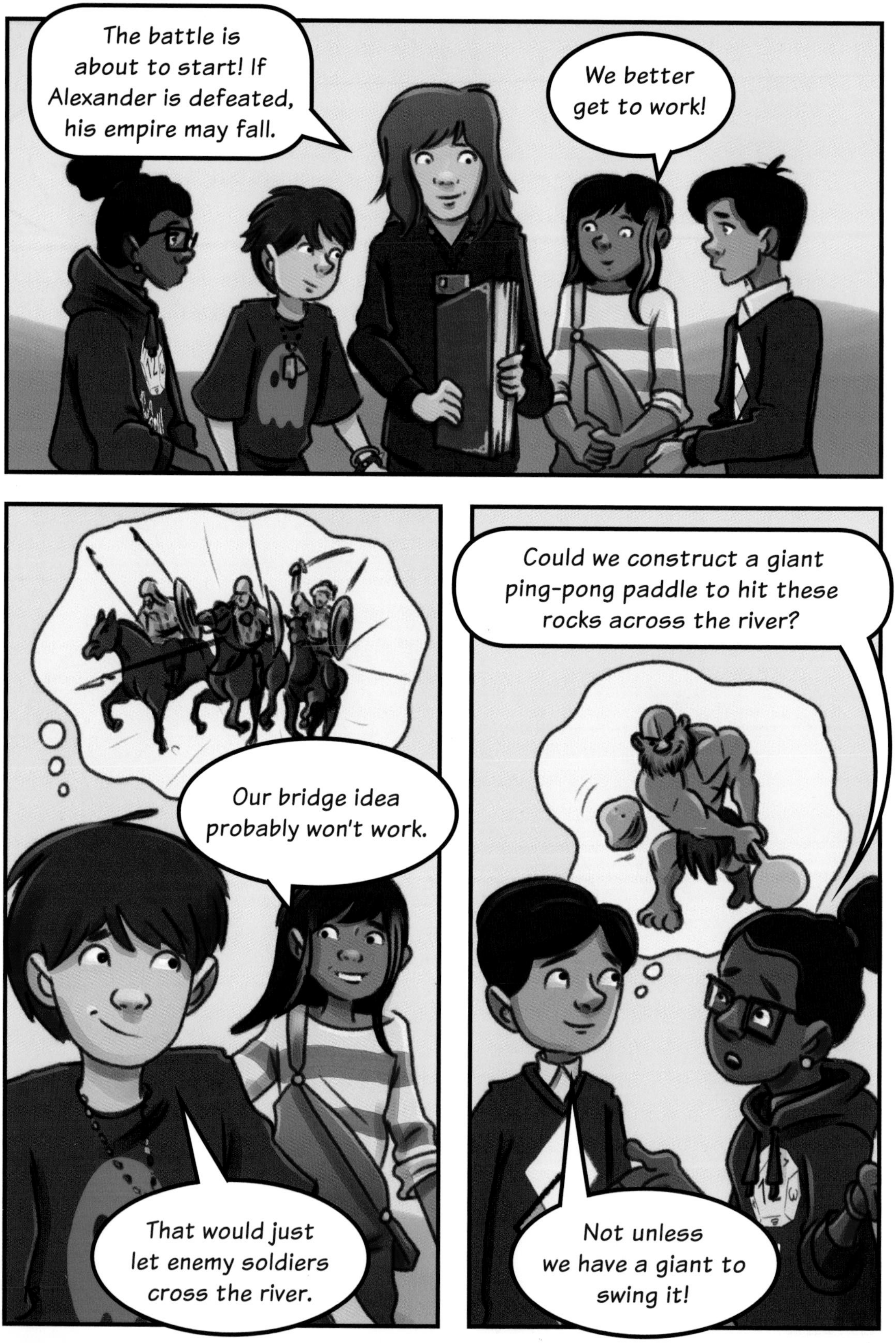
The battle is about to start! If Alexander is defeated, his empire may fall.
We better get to work!
Our bridge idea probably won't work.
That would just let enemy soldiers cross the river.
Could we construct a giant ping-pong paddle to hit these rocks across the river?
Not unless we have a giant to swing it!

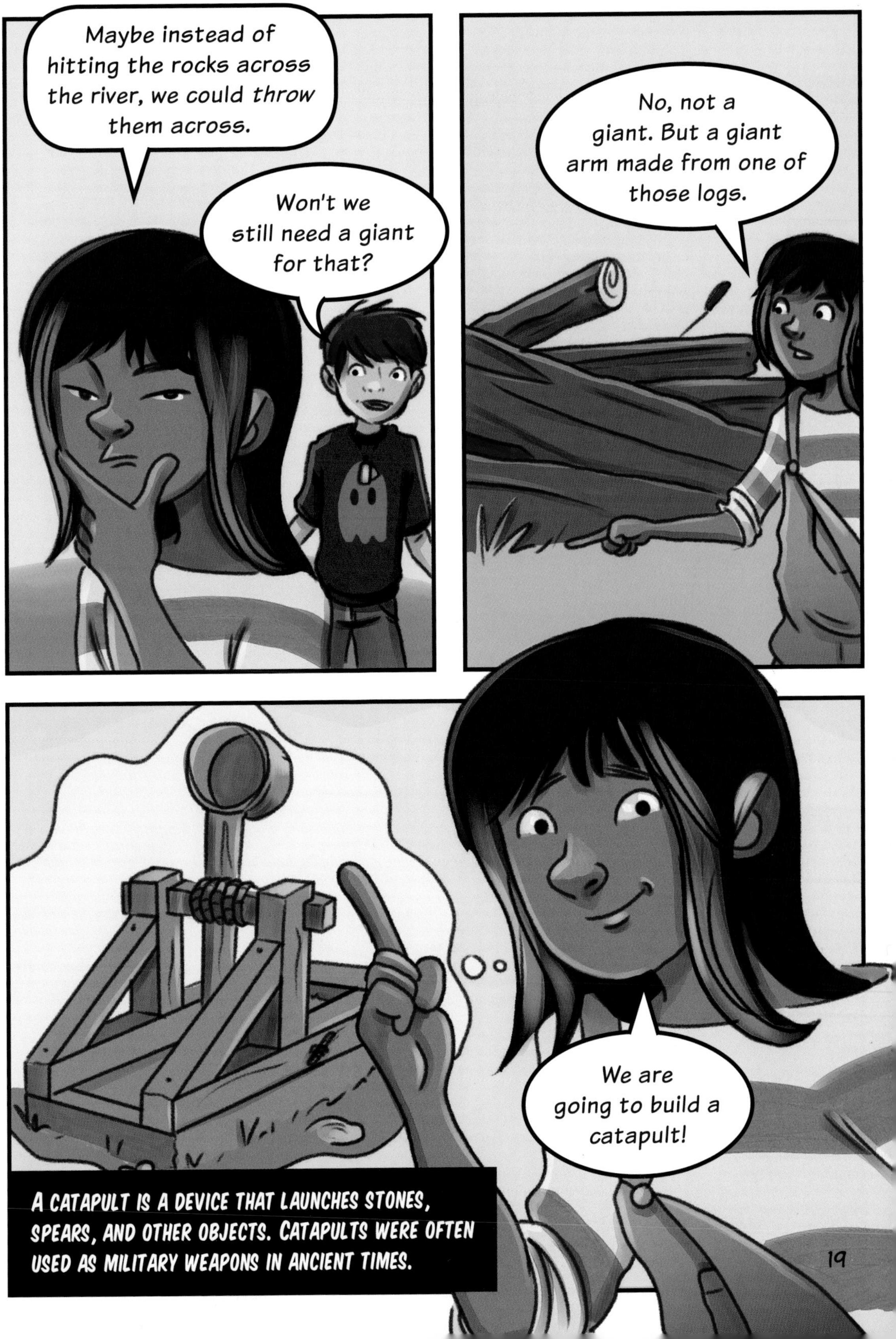

Maybe instead of hitting the rocks across the river, we could *throw* them across.
Won't we still need a giant for that?
No, not a giant. But a giant arm made from one of those logs.
We are going to build a catapult!
A CATAPULT IS A DEVICE THAT LAUNCHES STONES, SPEARS, AND OTHER OBJECTS. CATAPULTS WERE OFTEN USED AS MILITARY WEAPONS IN ANCIENT TIMES.

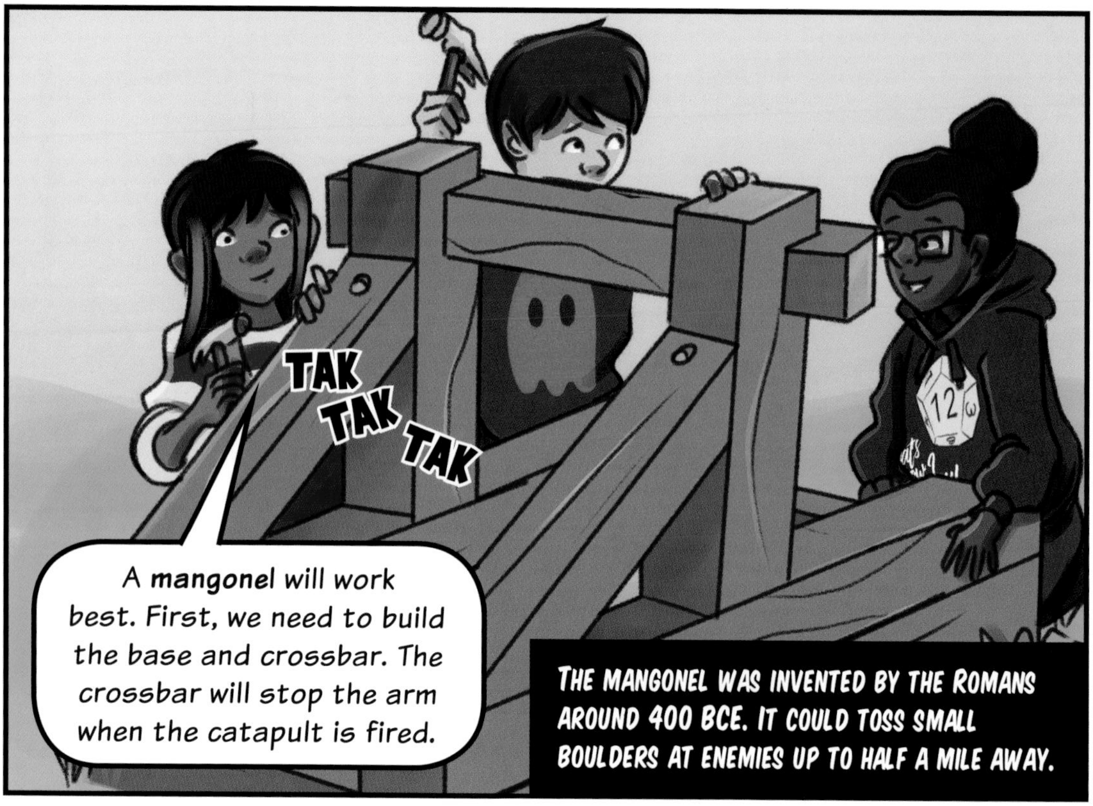
TAK TAK TAK
A mangonel will work best. First, we need to build the base and crossbar. The crossbar will stop the arm when the catapult is fired.
THE MANGONEL WAS INVENTED BY THE ROMANS AROUND 400 BCE. IT COULD TOSS SMALL BOULDERS AT ENEMIES UP TO HALF A MILE AWAY.

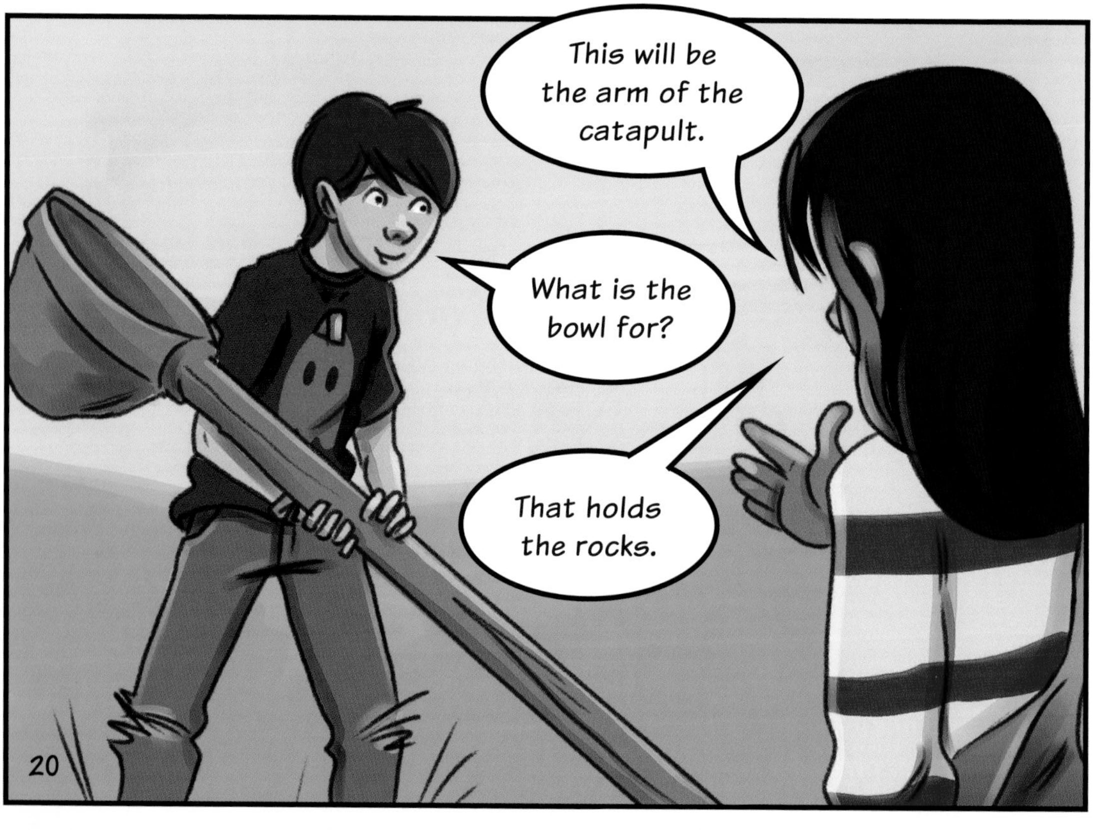
This will be the arm of the catapult.
What is the bowl for?
That holds the rocks.

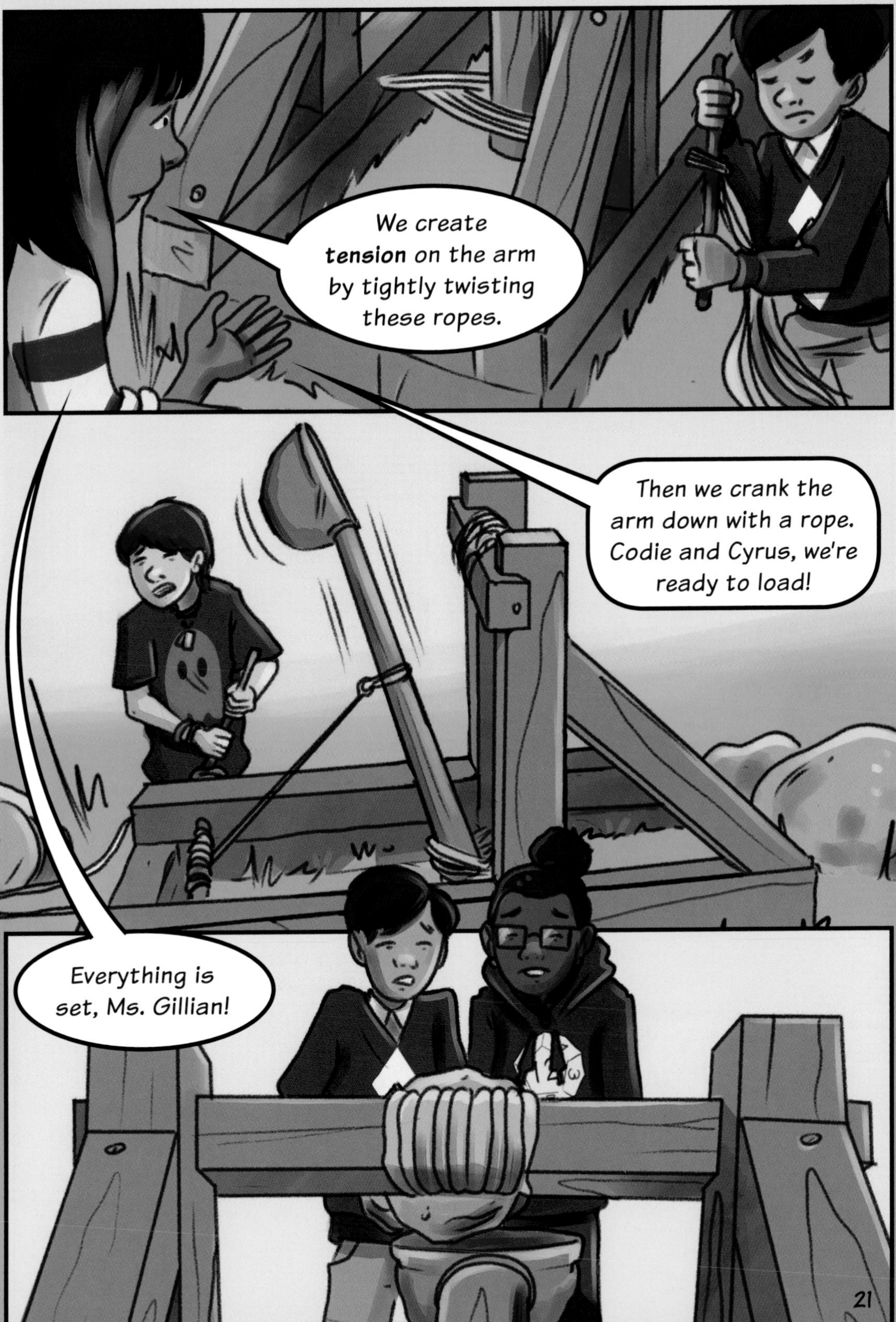

We create **tension** on the arm by tightly twisting these ropes.
Then we crank the arm down with a rope. Codie and Cyrus, we're ready to load!
Everything is set, Ms. Gillian!

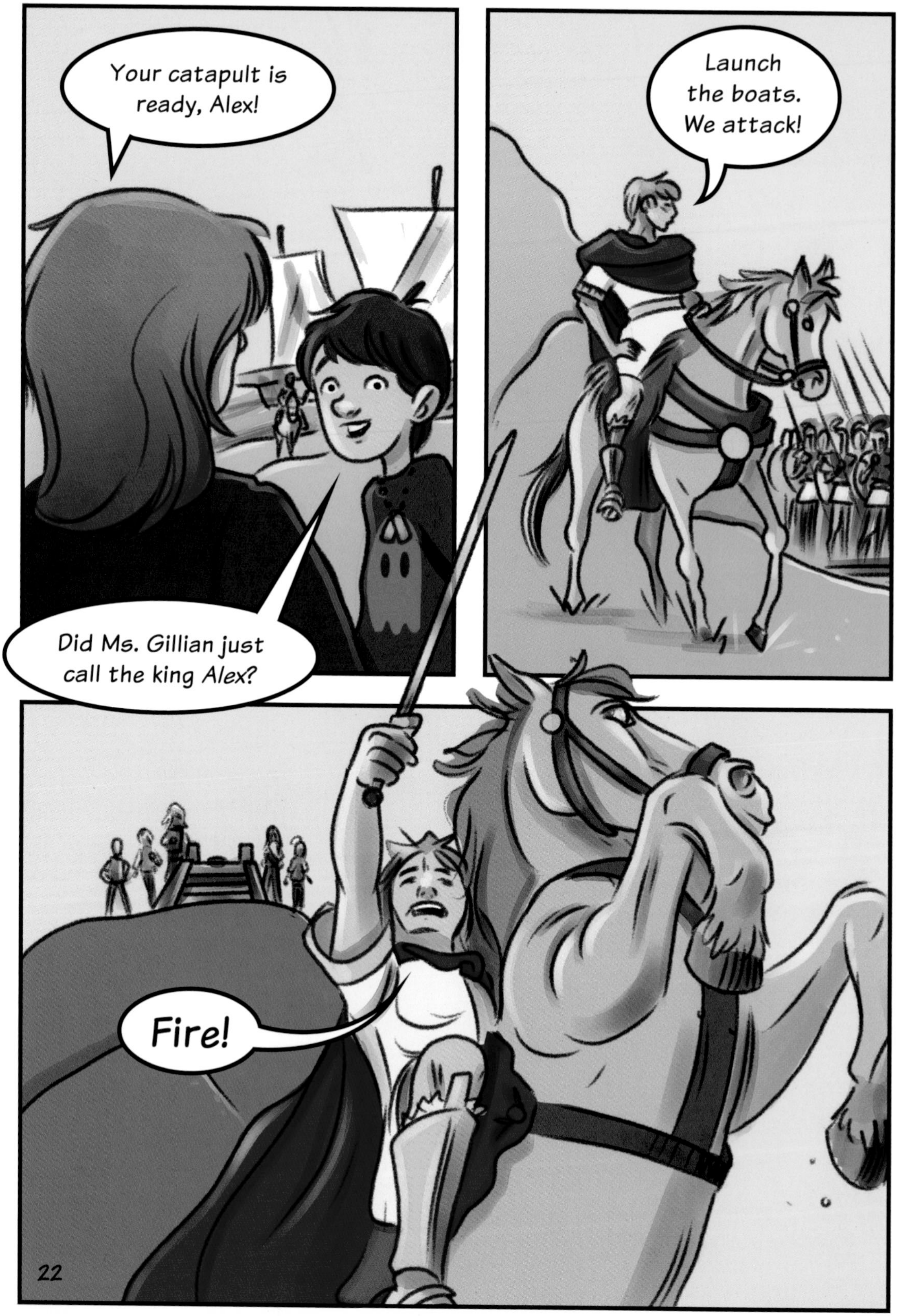
Your catapult is ready, Alex!
Did Ms. Gillian just call the king *Alex*?
Launch the boats. We attack!
Fire!

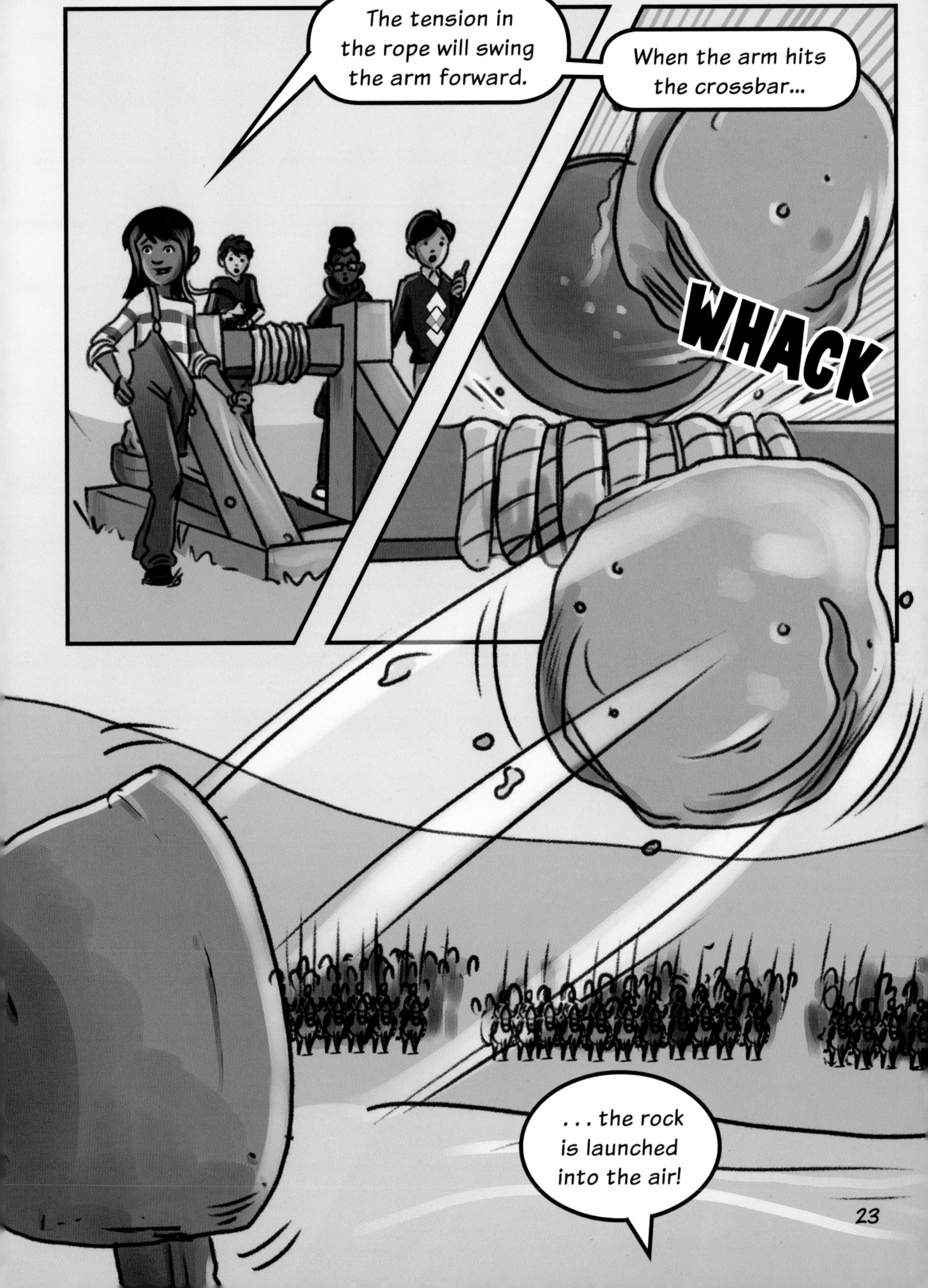
The tension in the rope will swing the arm forward.
When the arm hits the crossbar...
WHACK
. . . the rock is launched into the air!

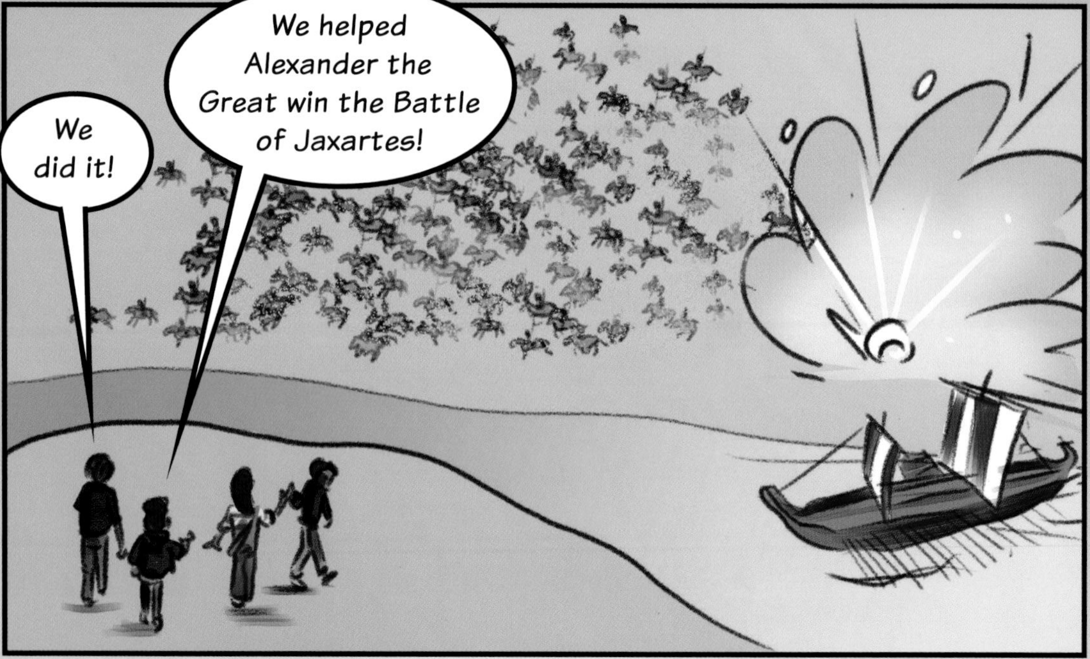
We did it!
We helped Alexander the Great win the Battle of Jaxartes!

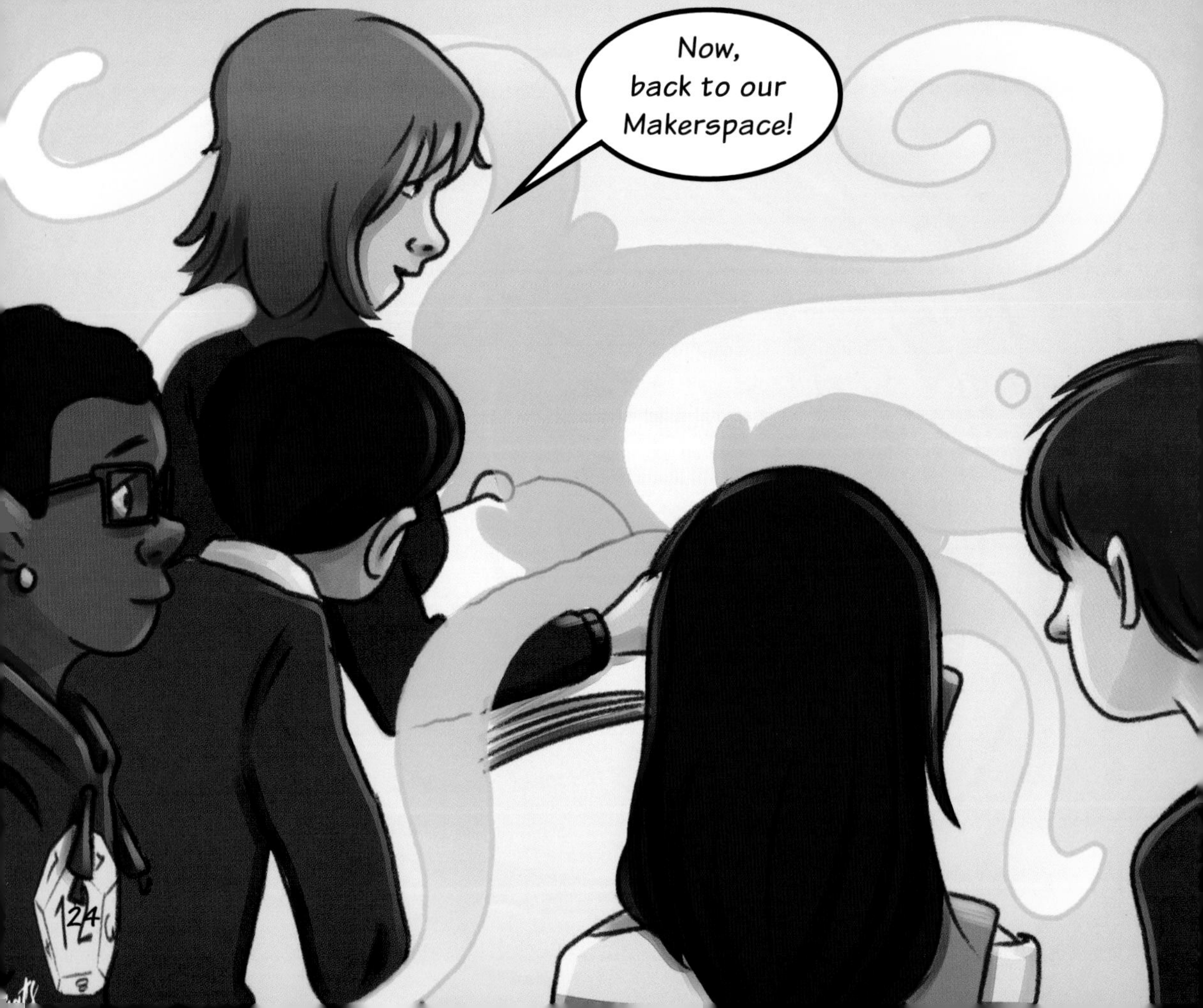
Now, back to our Makerspace!

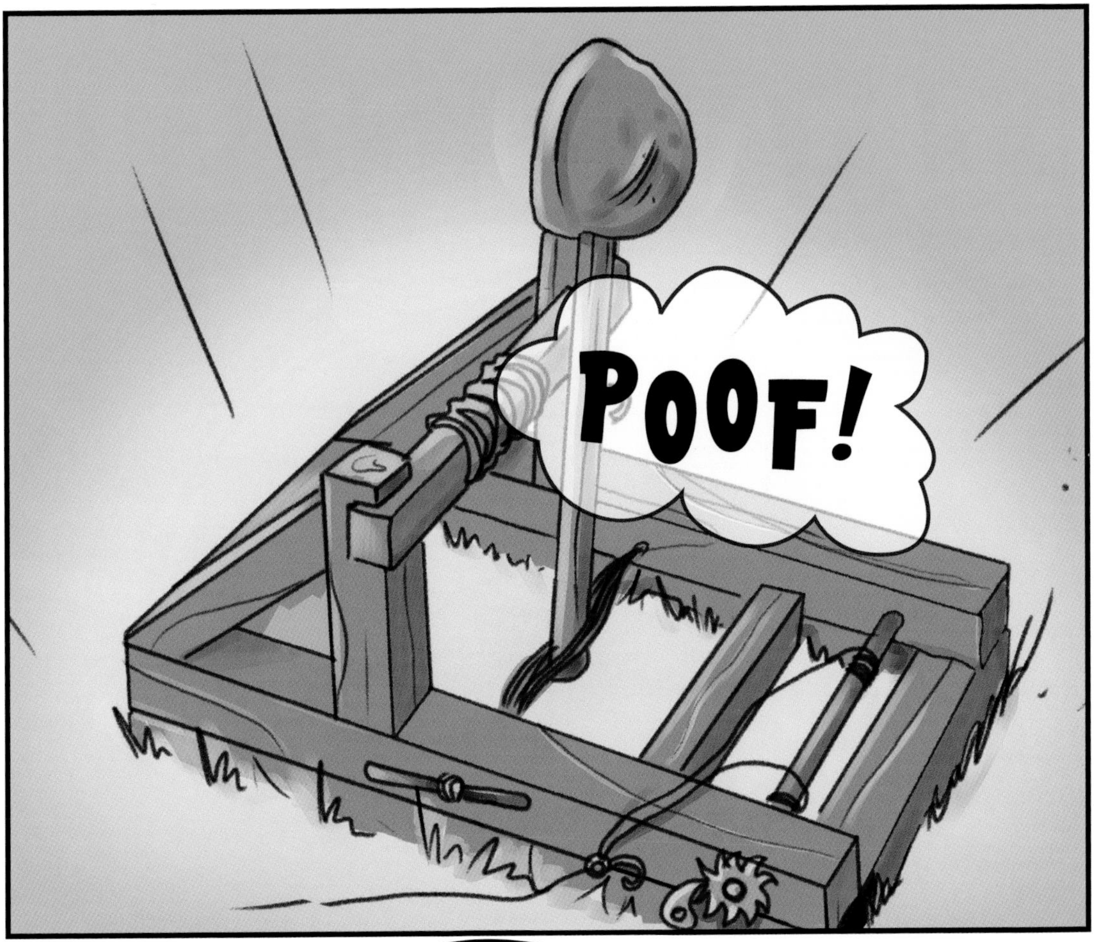
POOF!

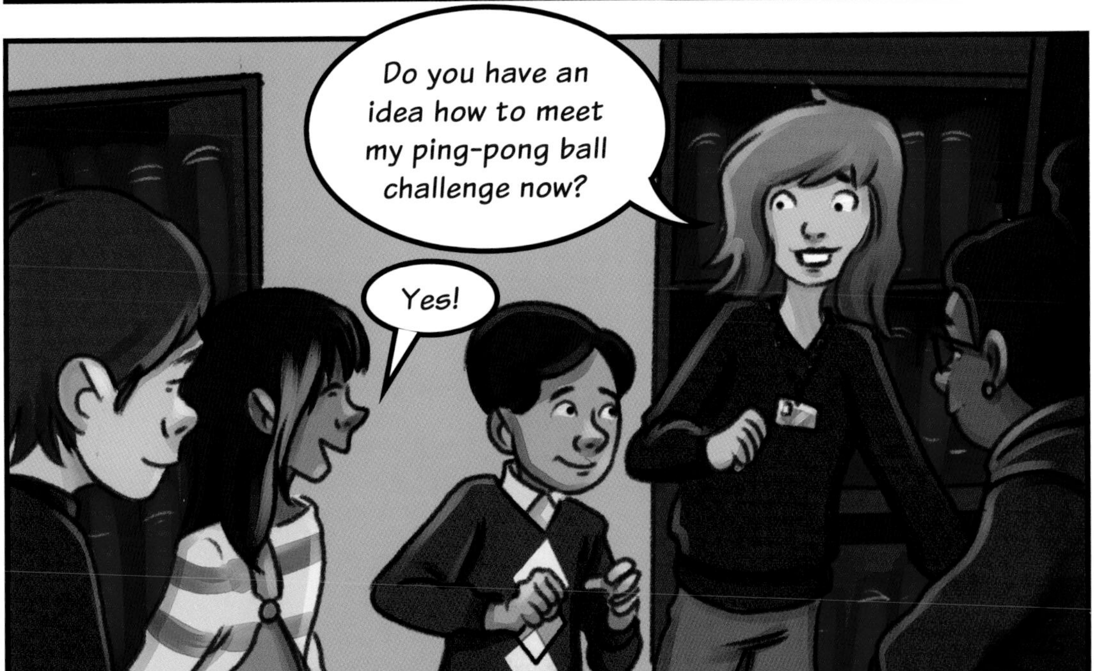
Do you have an idea how to meet my ping-pong ball challenge now?
Yes!

CATAPULT CLASH

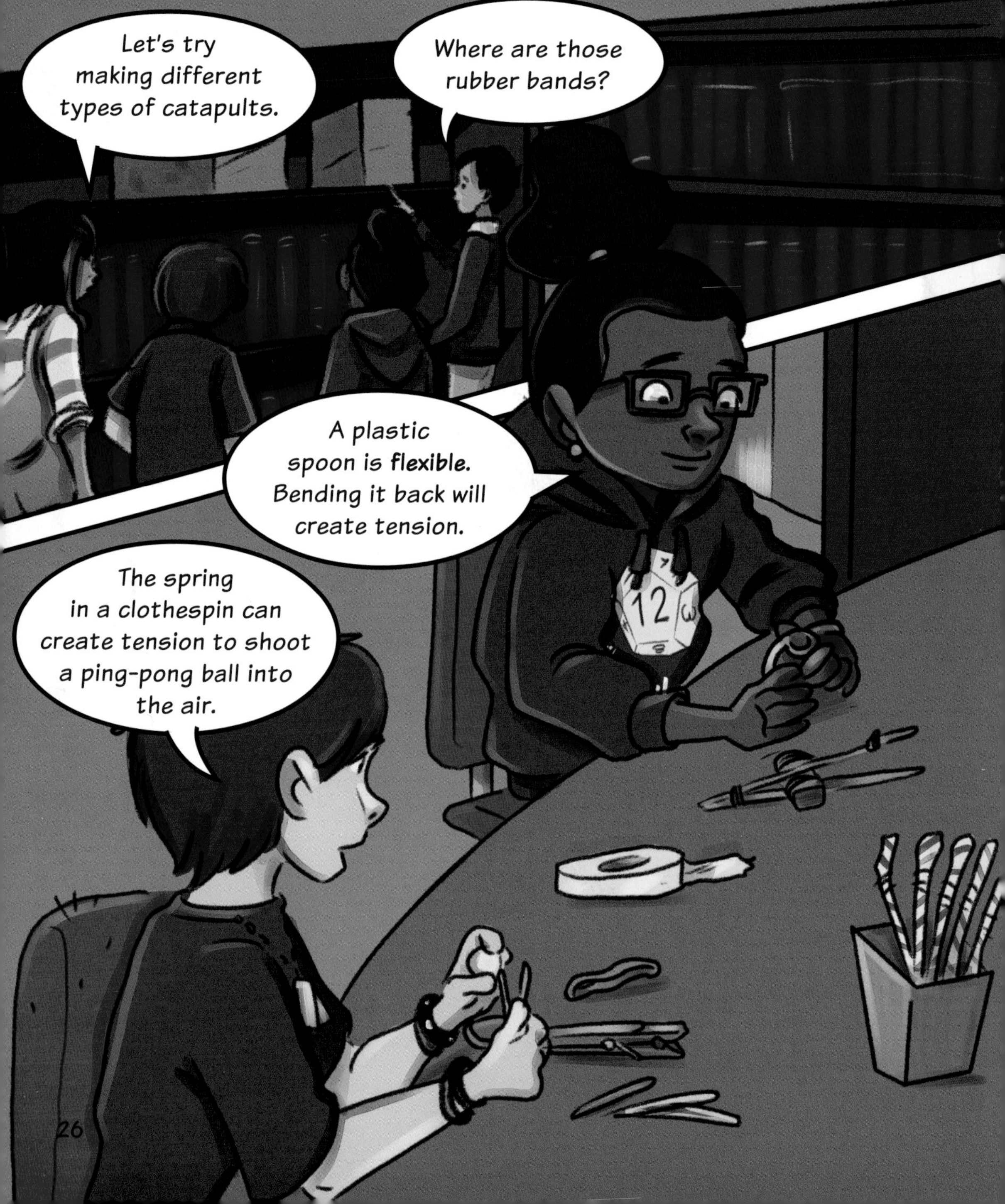
Let's try making different types of catapults.
Where are those rubber bands?
A plastic spoon is **flexible.** Bending it back will create tension.
The spring in a clothespin can create tension to shoot a ping-pong ball into the air.

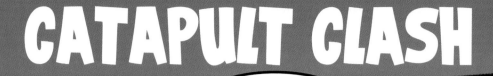

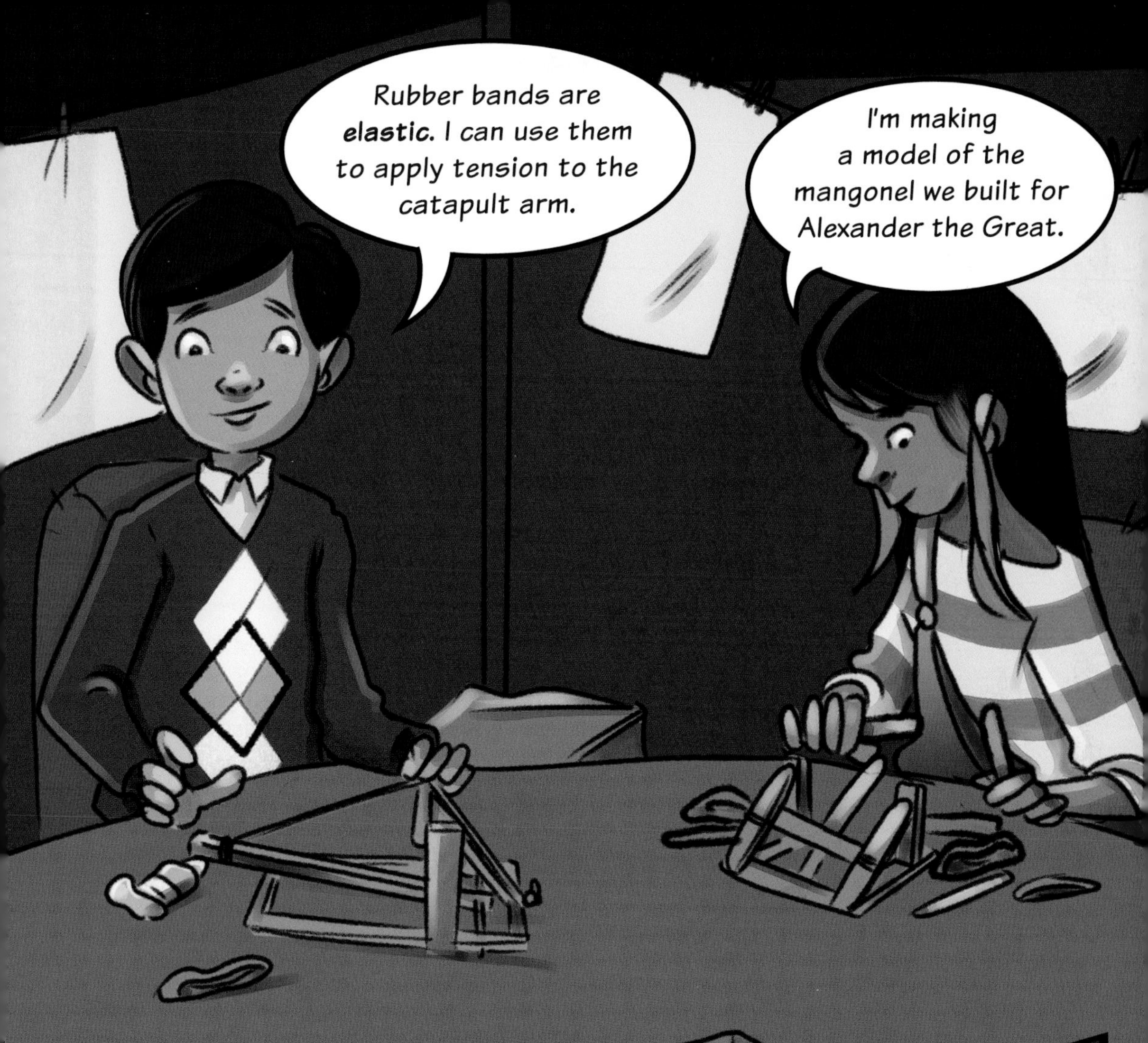
Rubber bands are **elastic.** I can use them to apply tension to the catapult arm.
I'm making a model of the mangonel we built for Alexander the Great.

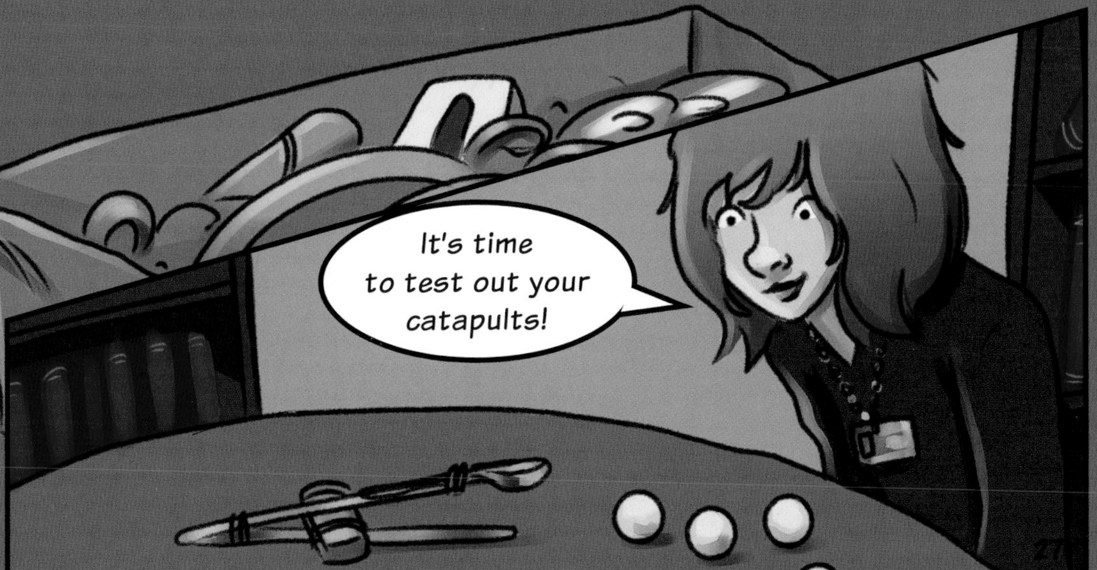
It's time to test out your catapults!

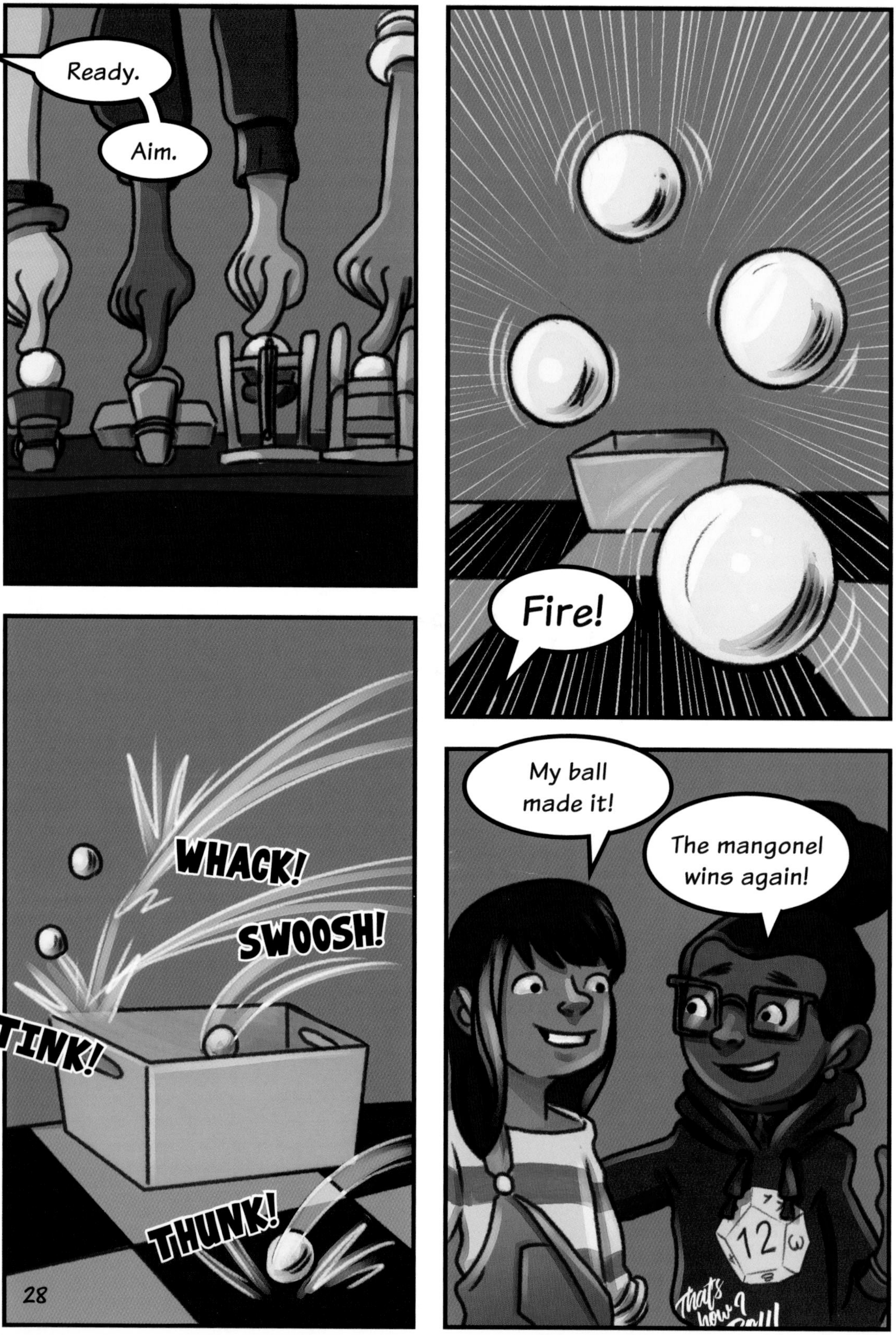
Ready.
Aim.
Fire!
WHACK!
SWOOSH!
TINK!
THUNK!
My ball made it!
The mangonel wins again!

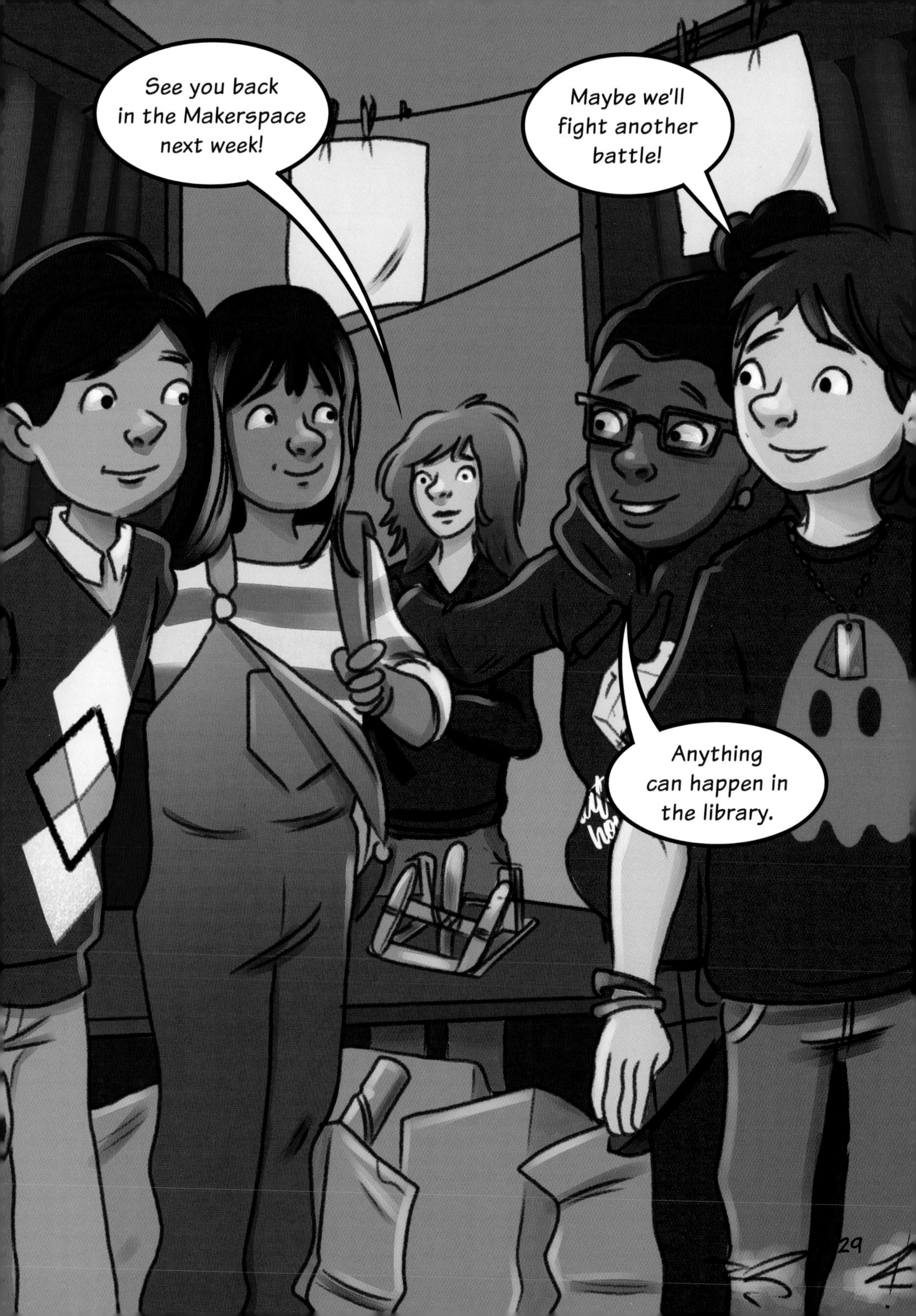
See you back in the Makerspace next week!
Maybe we'll fight another battle!
Anything can happen in the library.

GLOSSARY

elastic—able to stretch and then return to its original shape

flexible—able to easily bend

hovercraft—vehicle that travels on a cushion of flowing air

logic—system of thinking through problems, often by showing how facts are related

mangonel (MAN-guh-nel)—ancient type of catapult

philosopher—person who thinks about the world and searches for wisdom

strategy—art of making plans in order to achieve a goal

tension—stiffness from being stretched

CREATE YOUR OWN MAKERSPACE!

1. Find a place to store supplies. It could be a large area, like the space in this story. But it can also be a cart, bookshelf, or storage bin.

2. Make a list of supplies that you would like to have. Include items found in your recycling bin, such as cardboard boxes, tin cans, and plastic bottles (caps too!). Add art materials, household items such as rubber bands, paper clips, straws, and any other materials useful for planning, building, and creating.

3. Pass out your list to friends and parents. Ask them for help in gathering the materials.

4. It's time to create. Let your imagination run wild!

BUILD A CATAPULT!

WHAT YOU NEED

- Nine wide craft sticks
- Rubber bands
- Plastic spoon
- Marshmallows or ping-pong balls

There are many ways to build a catapult. The key in any design is creating tension on the arm of the catapult. These steps show how to make a catapult like the one Codie built on page 26.

1. MAKE THE BASE OF THE CATAPULT. Stack seven craft sticks on top of one another. Wrap rubber bands around each end of the stack to hold the sticks together.

2. MAKE THE CATAPULT BOWL. Stack the spoon handle along the length of one of the remaining craft sticks, with the bowl sticking off the end. Wrap one or two rubber bands tightly around the craft stick to hold the spoon in place.

3. MAKE THE CATAPULT ARM. Stack the stick with the spoon on top of the remaining craft stick. Wrap a rubber band tightly around the end of the stack opposite the spoon bowl.

4. CONNECT THE CATAPULT ARM TO THE BASE. Carefully slide the base between the two craft sticks of the arm, making a t shape with the spoon on top.

5. FIRE AWAY! Place a marshmallow or ping-pong ball in the spoon and then pull it back. The flexibility of the spoon will create tension. Once you let it go, the catapult arm will swing forward and fling your ammunition through the air!

Now try building catapults like the ones Eliza, Matt, and Cyrus make on pages 26 and 27. Test them out. Which one flings objects the farthest?

FURTHER RESOURCES

Ives, Rob. *Break the Siege: Make Your Own Catapults*. Minneapolis: Hungry Tomato, 2017.

Miller, Shannon McClintock, and Blake Hoena. *A Robotics Mission*. North Mankato, MN: Capstone, 2019.

Miller, Tim, and Rebecca Sjonger. *Levers in My Makerspace*. New York: Crabtree, 2017.

Waterfield, Kathryn. *Who Was Alexander the Great?* New York: Grosset & Dunlap, 2016.